Best Buddies

A Pie for Us!

Written by
Vicky Fang

Art by
Luisa Leal

ACORN™
SCHOLASTIC INC.

For Constantin, who loves pie. — VF

To my best friend, Nali. — LL

Text copyright © 2023 by Vicky Fang
Illustrations copyright © 2023 by Luisa Leal

Library of Congress Cataloging-in-Publication Data

Names: Fang, Vicky, author. | Leal, Luisa, illustrator.
Title: A pie for us! / written by Vicky Fang ; illustrated by Luisa Leal.
Description: First edition. | New York : Acorn/Scholastic, Inc., 2023. | Series: Best Buddies; 1 | Audience: Ages 4–6. | Audience: Grades K–1. | Summary: Dog Sniff and cat Scratch live together in a house where sometimes they quarrel and sometimes they cooperate—especially when mischief is involved.
Identifiers: LCCN 2022016304 (print) | ISBN 9781338865578 (paperback) | ISBN 9781338865585 (library binding)
Subjects: LCSH: Dogs—Juvenile fiction. | Cats—Juvenile fiction. | Animal Behavior—Juvenile fiction. | CYAC: Dogs—Fiction. | Cats—Fiction. | Animals—Habits and behavior—Fiction. | LCGFT: Animal fiction. | Picture books.
Classification: LCC PZ7.1.F3543 Pi 2023 (print) | DDC [E]—dc23
LC record available at https://lccn.loc.gov/2022016304

10 9 8 7 6 5 4 3 2 1   23 24 25 26 27

Printed in China   62

First edition, October 2023
Edited by Katie Carella
Book design by Maria Mercado

The Pie

This is Sniff.

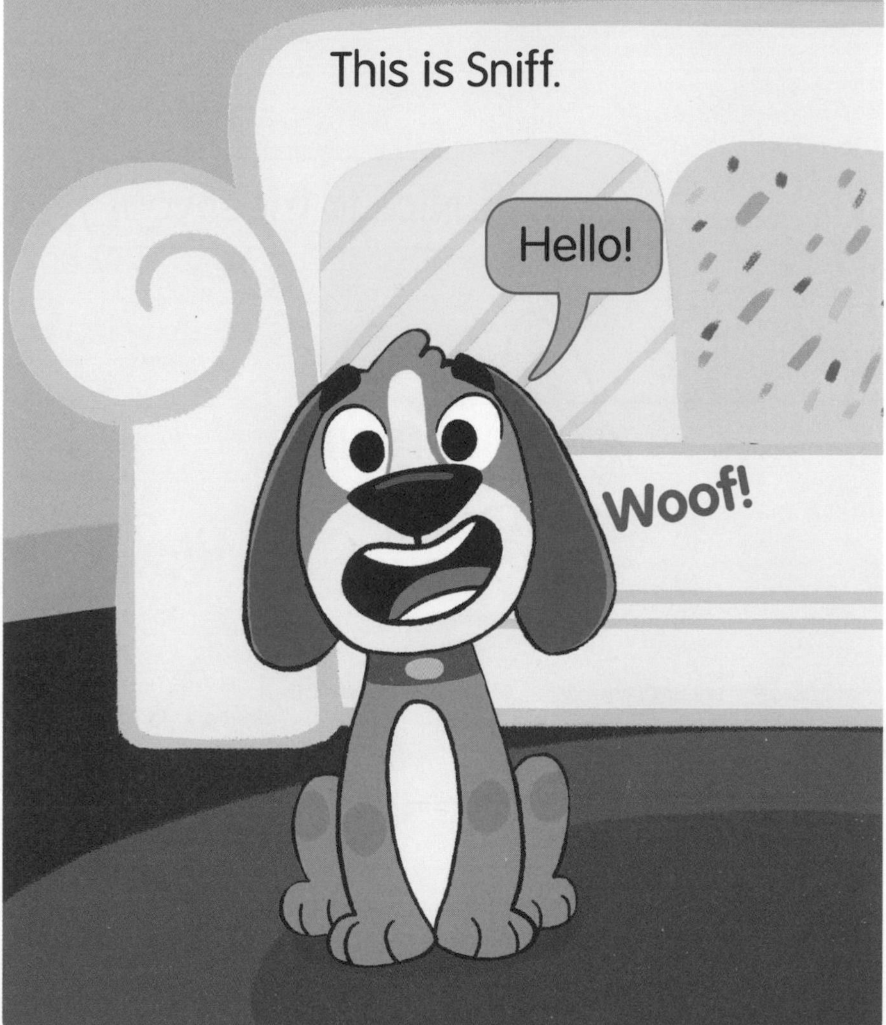
Hello!
Woof!

This is Scratch.

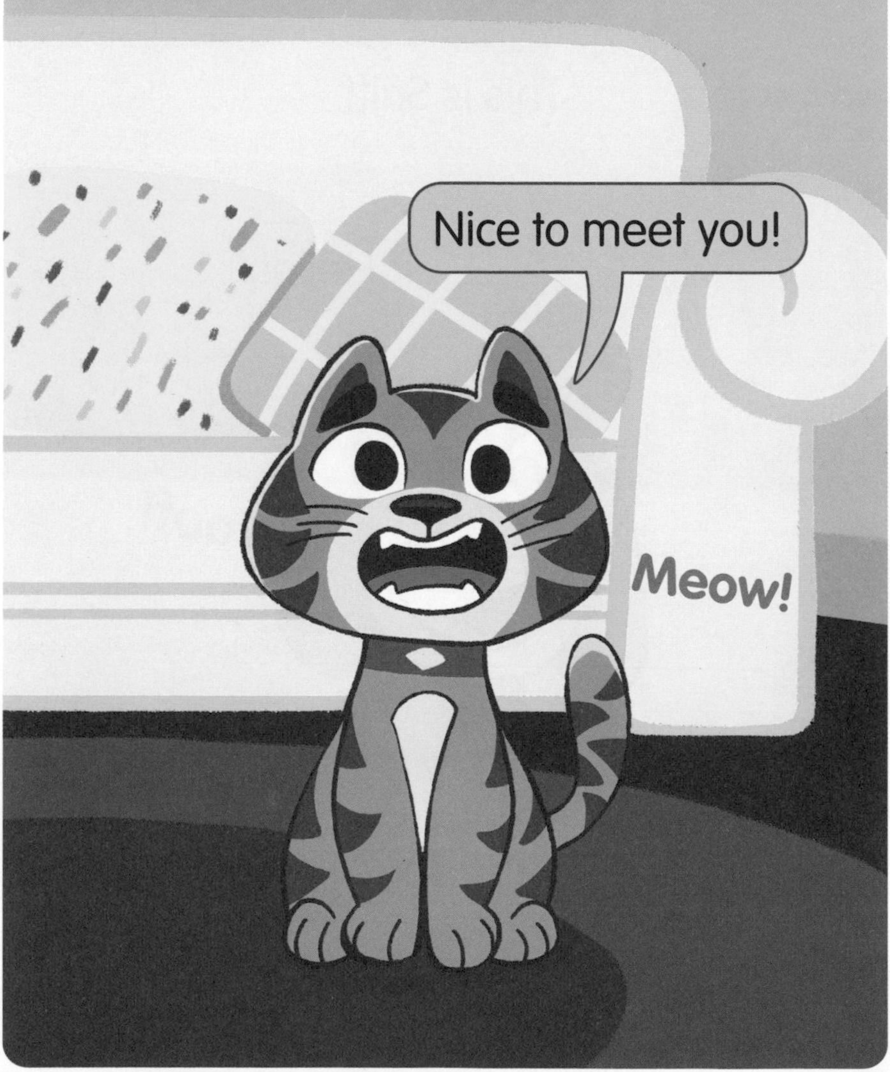
Nice to meet you!
Meow!

They are best buddies.

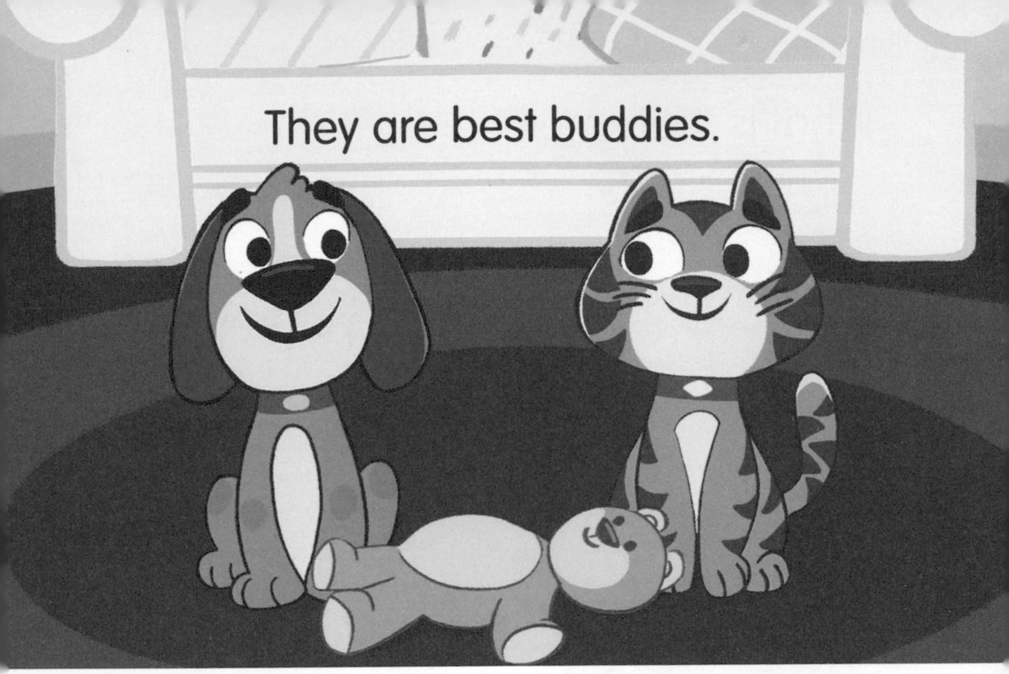

Well, sometimes.

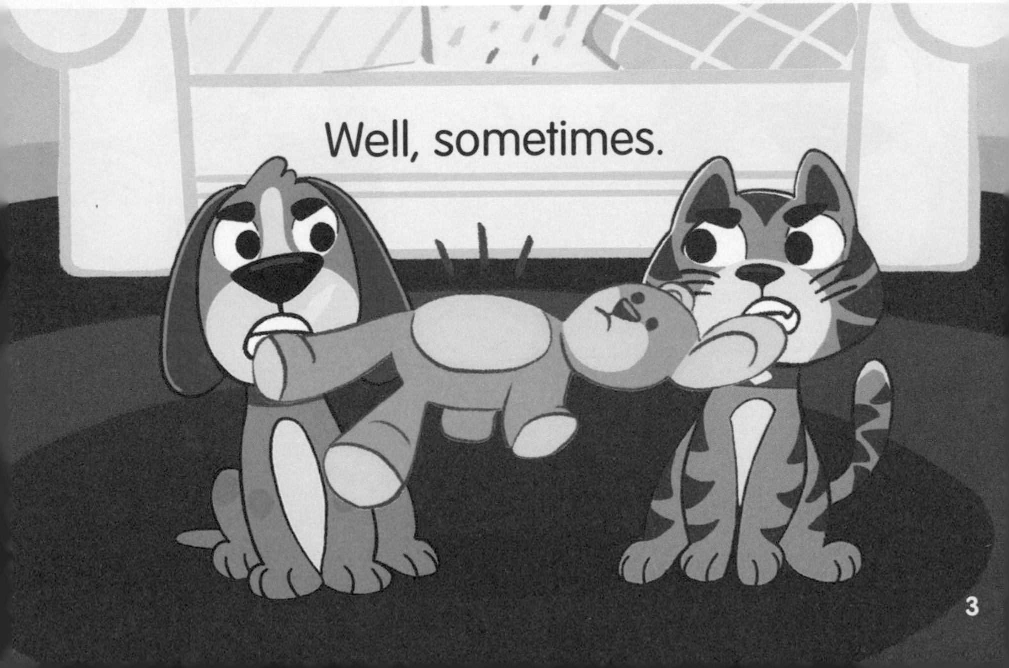

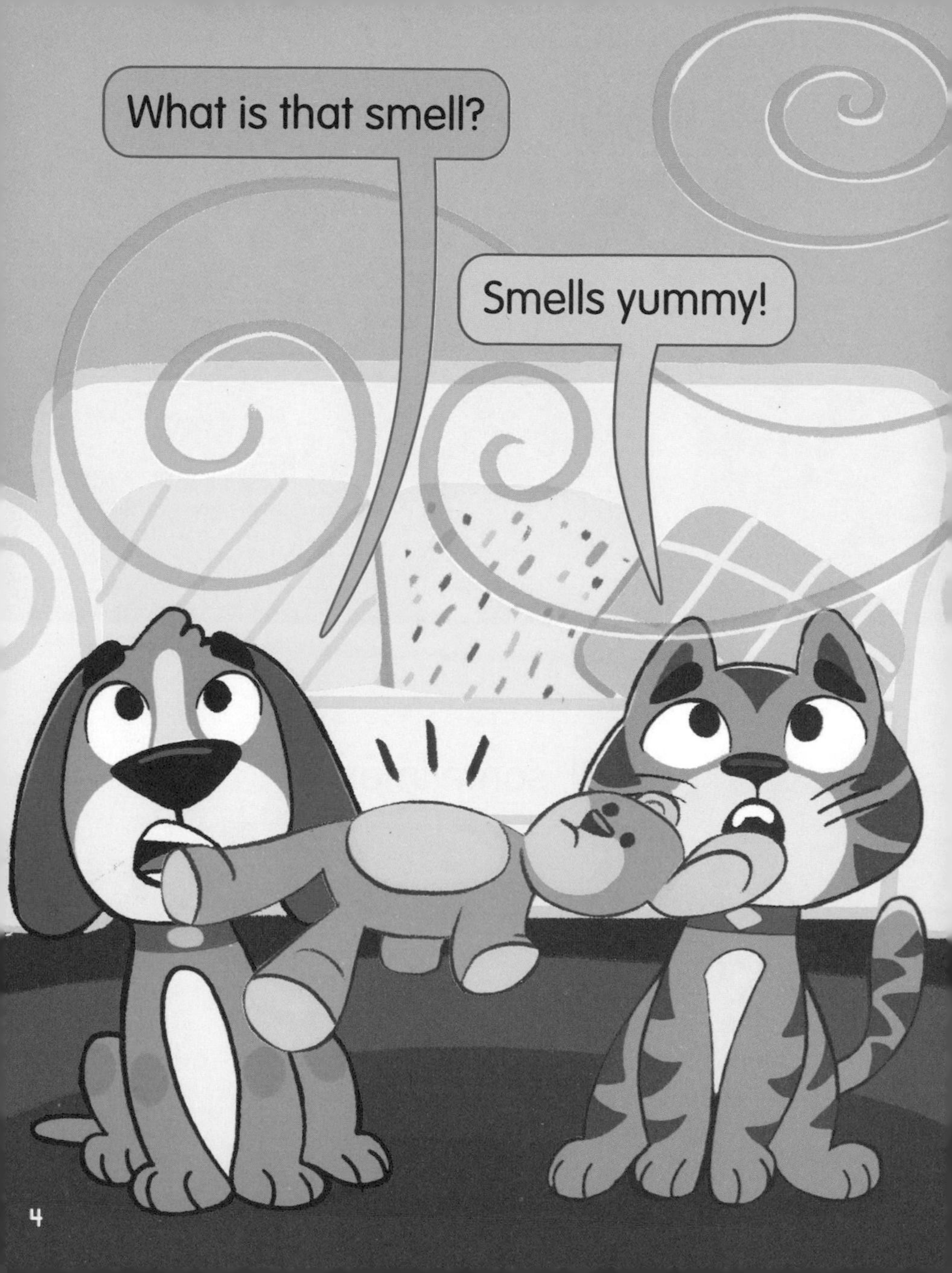
What is that smell?
Smells yummy!

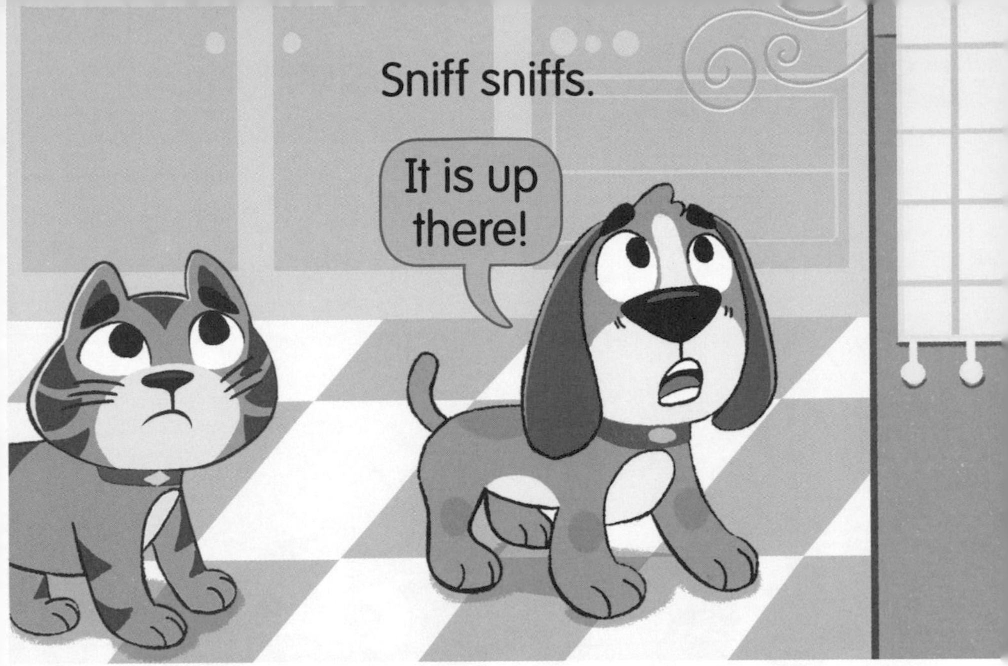
Sniff sniffs.
It is up there!

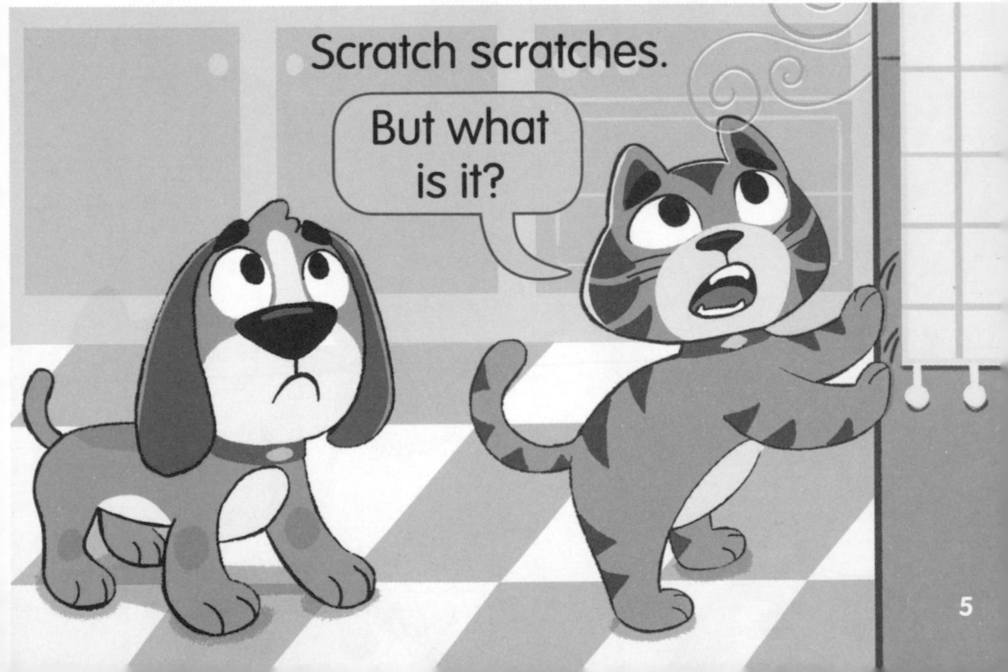
Scratch scratches.
But what is it?

Scratch jumps.

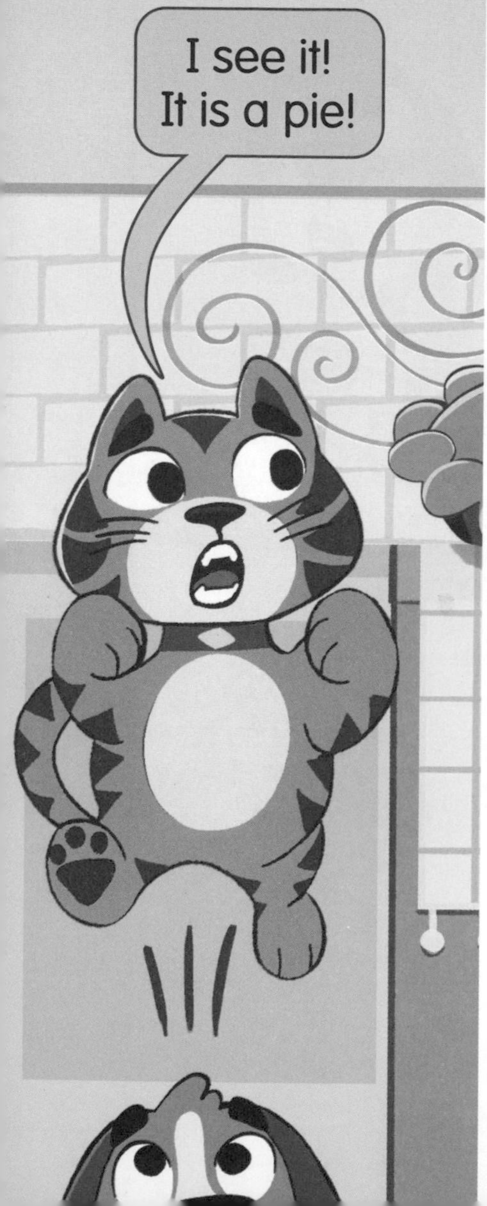
I see it!
It is a pie!

Sniff jumps.

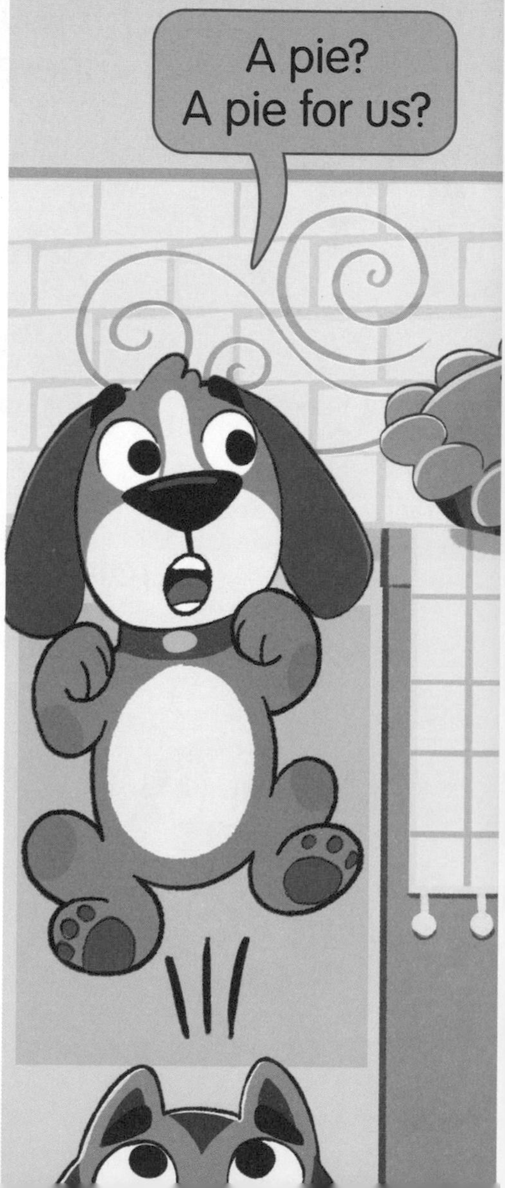
A pie?
A pie for us?

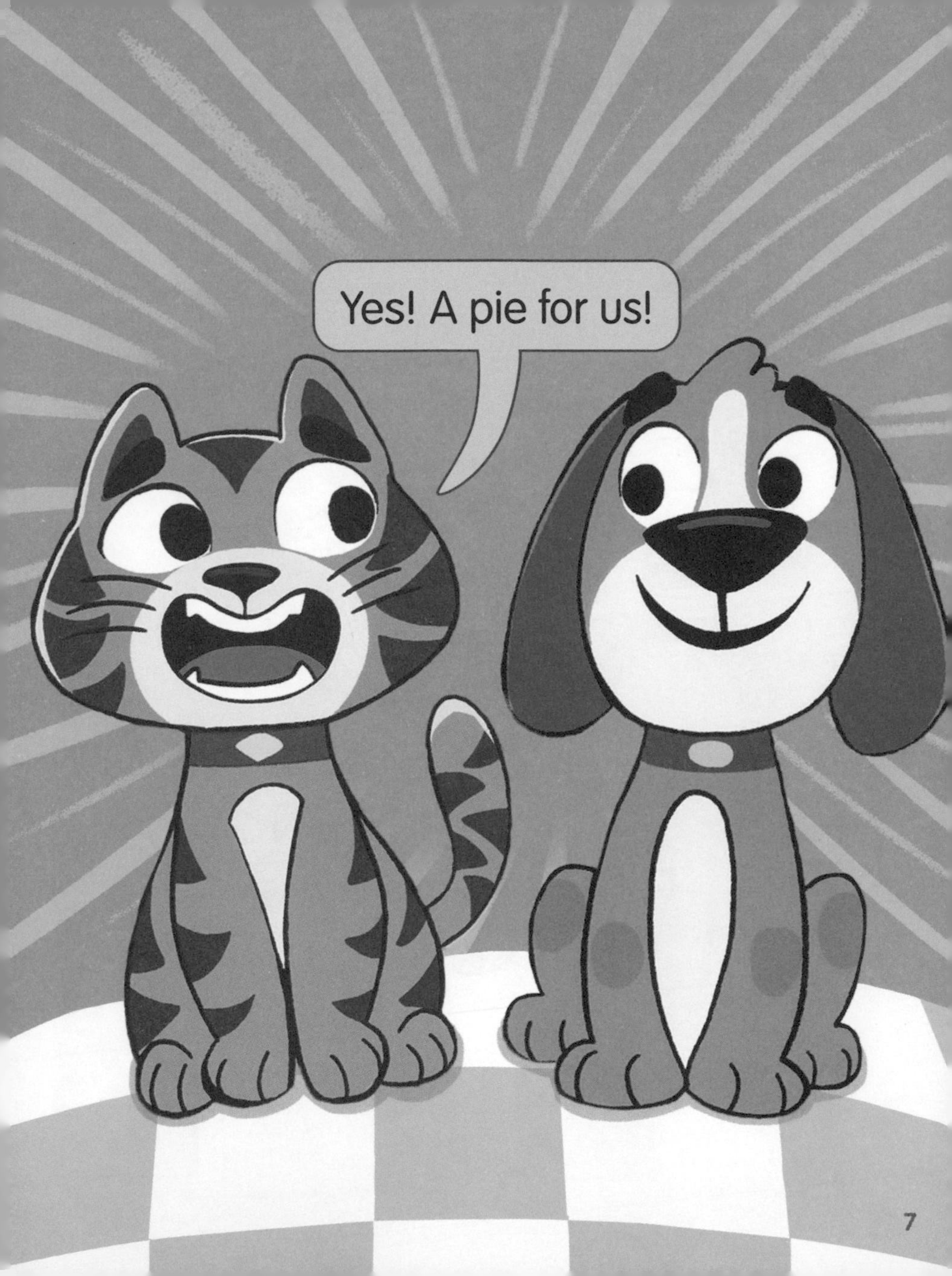
Yes! A pie for us!

Sniff and Scratch both jump.

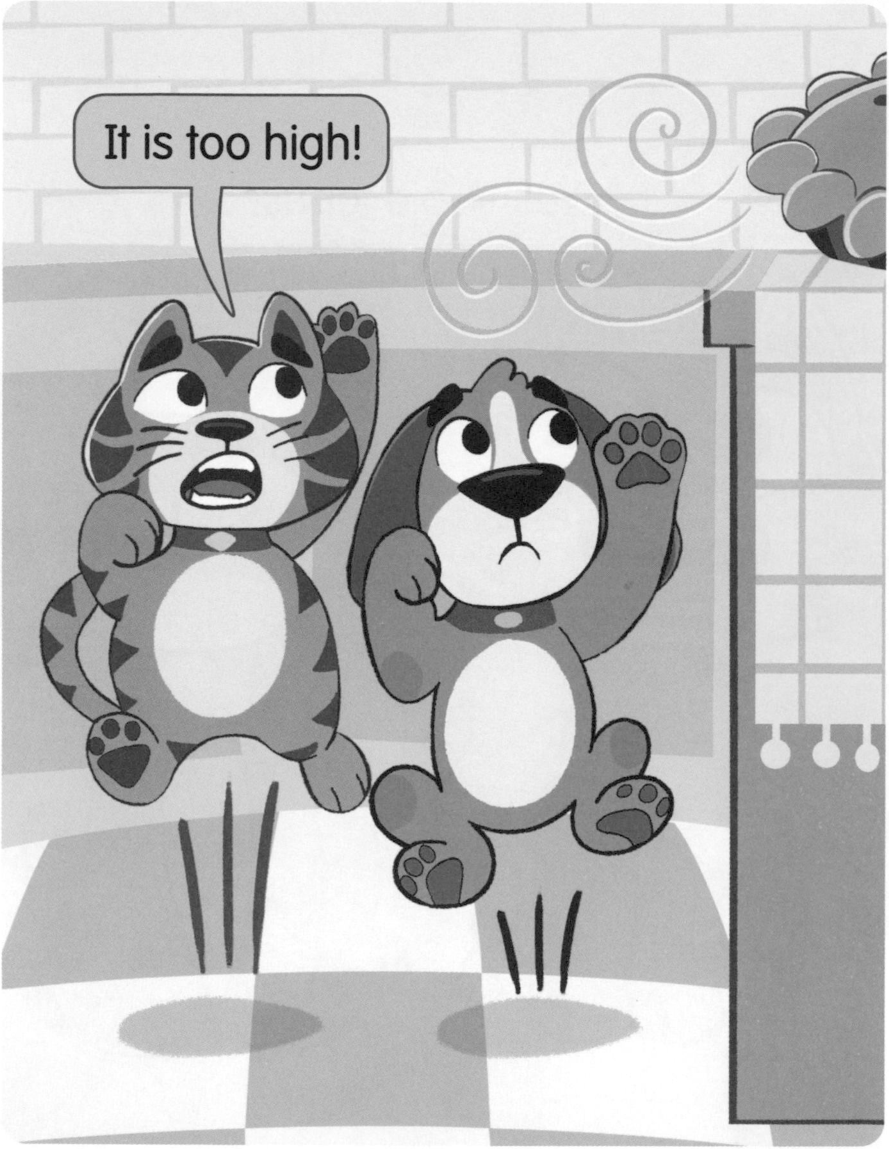
It is too high!

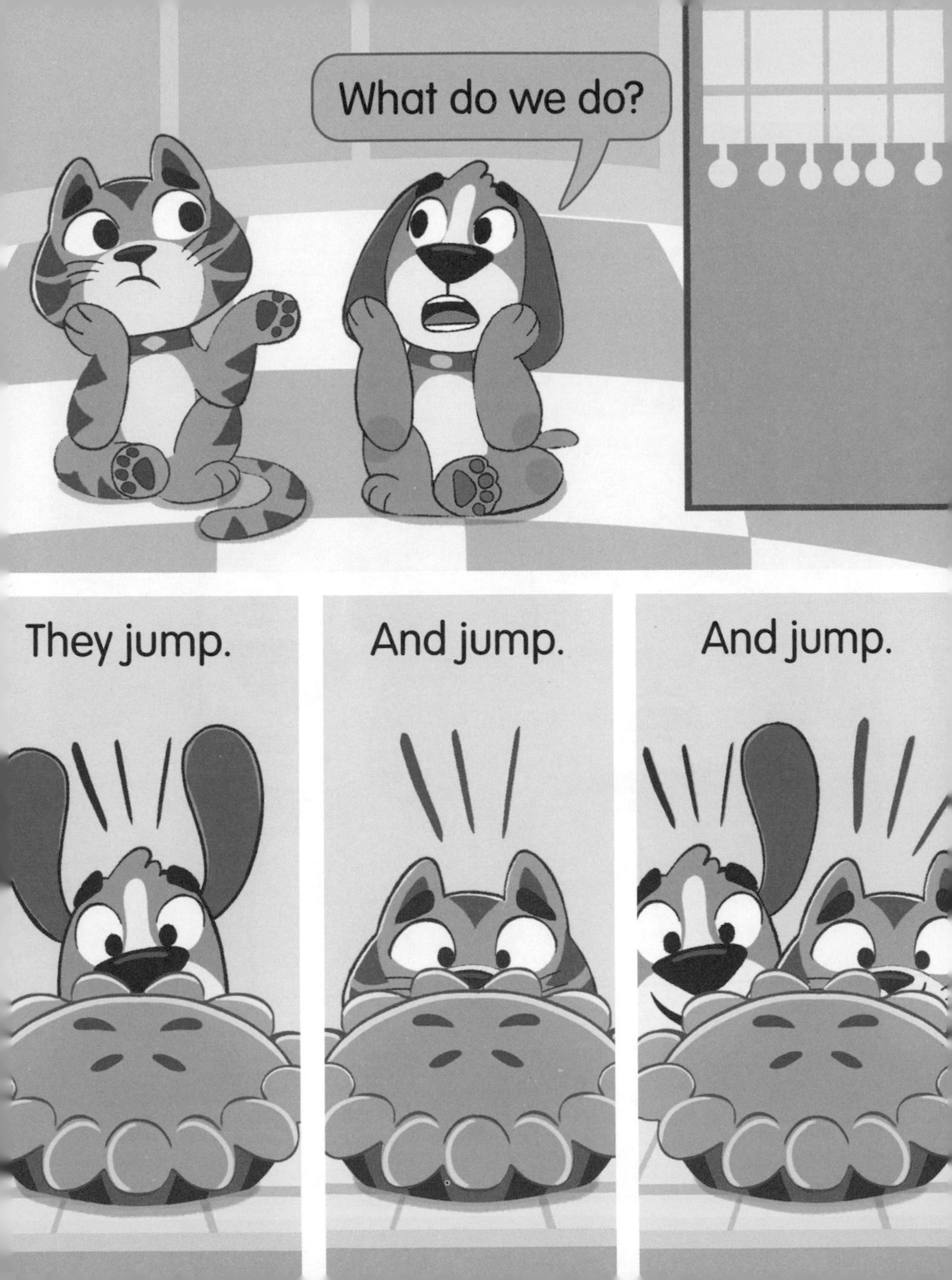
What do we do?
They jump.
And jump.
And jump.

They give up.

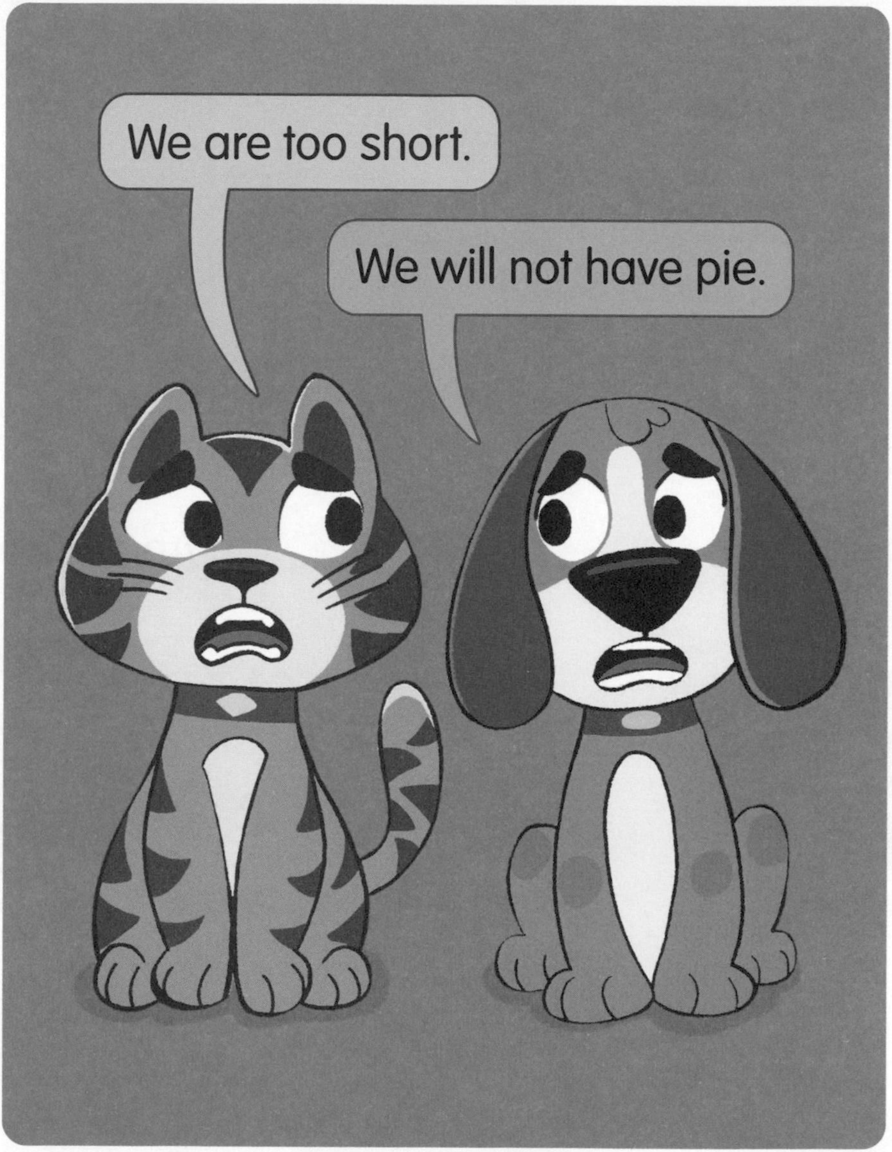
We are too short.
We will not have pie.

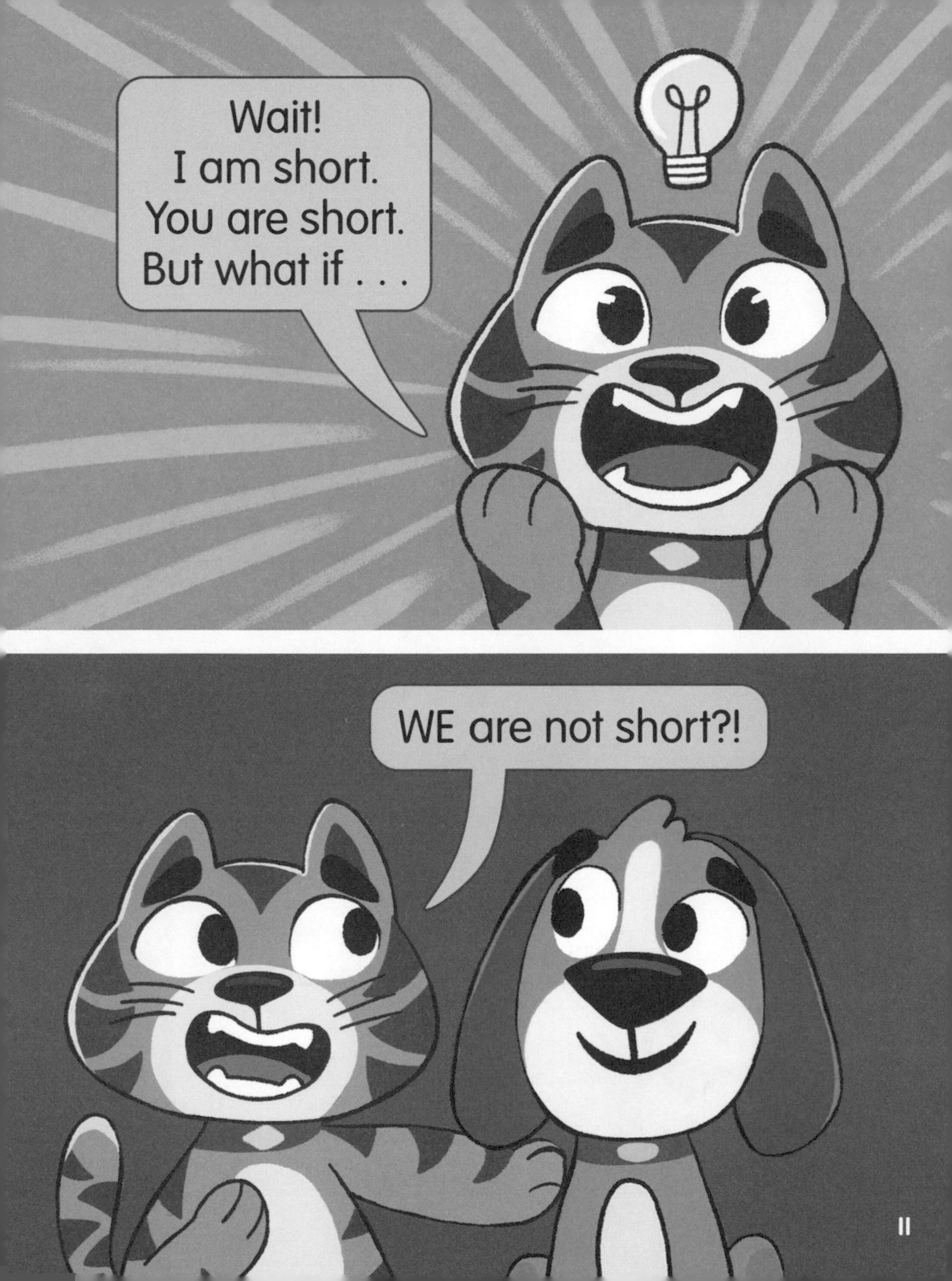
Wait!
I am short.
You are short.
But what if . . .
WE are not short?!

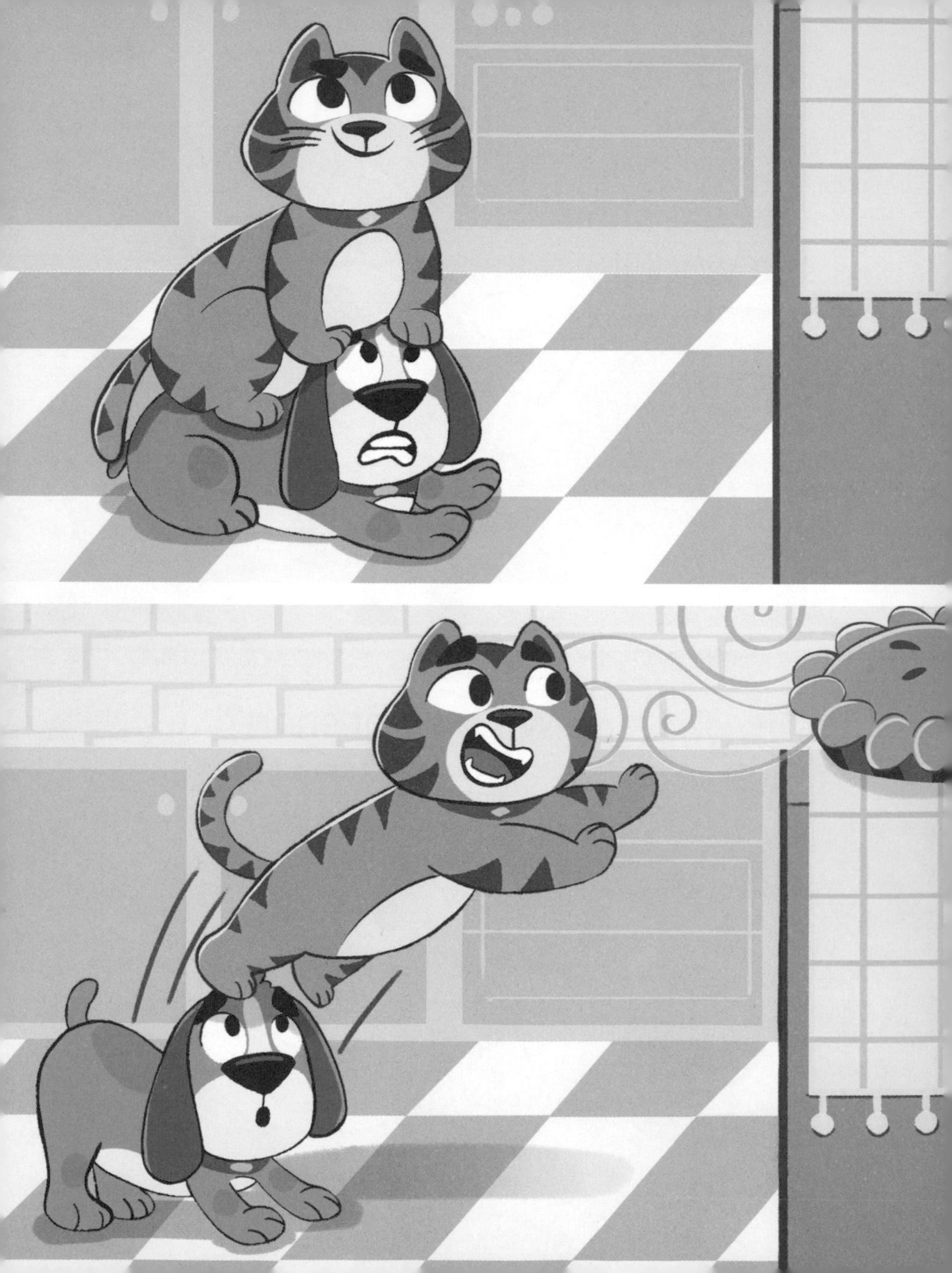

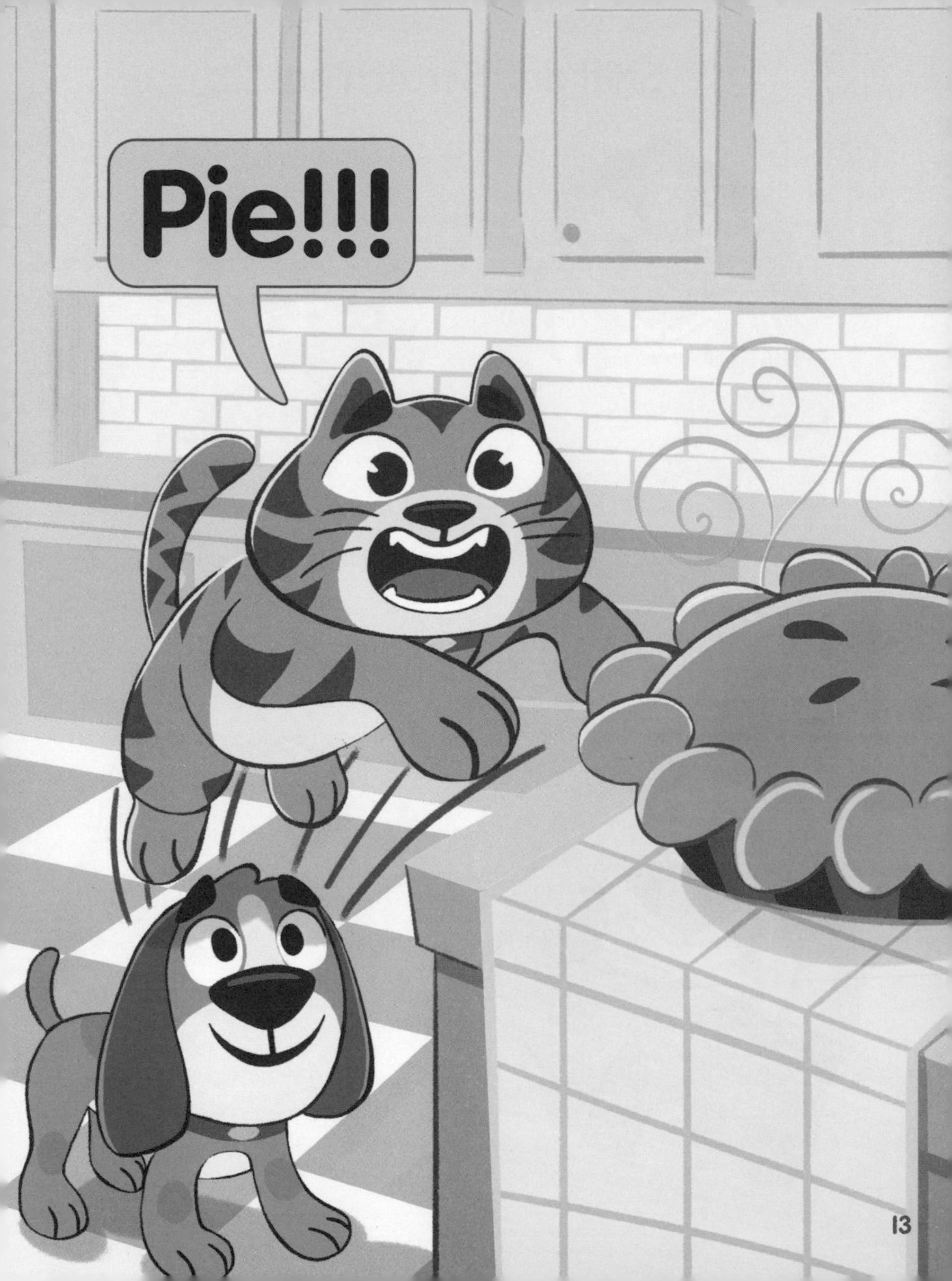
Pie!!!

Sniff and Scratch eat.

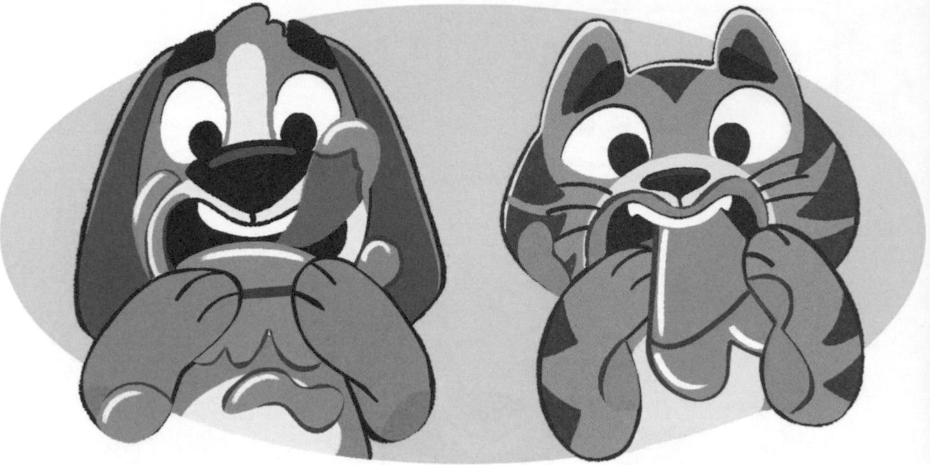

They eat and eat.

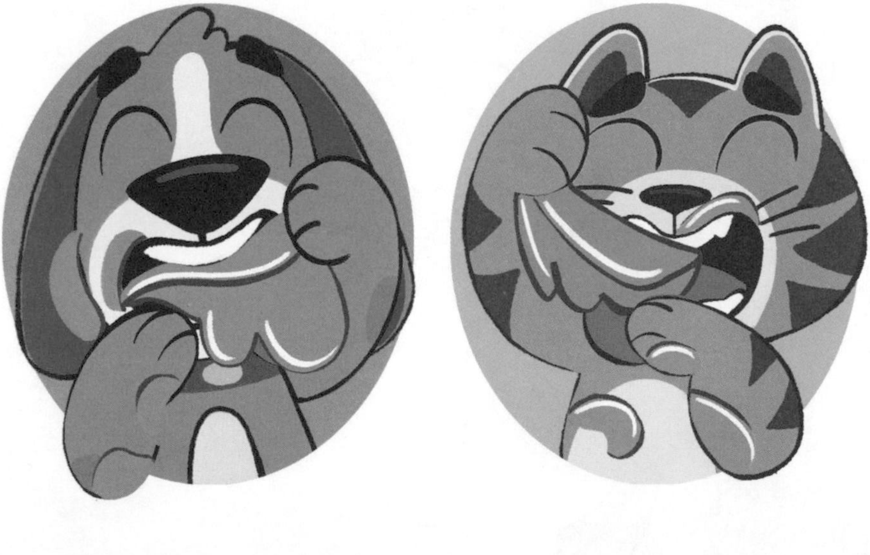

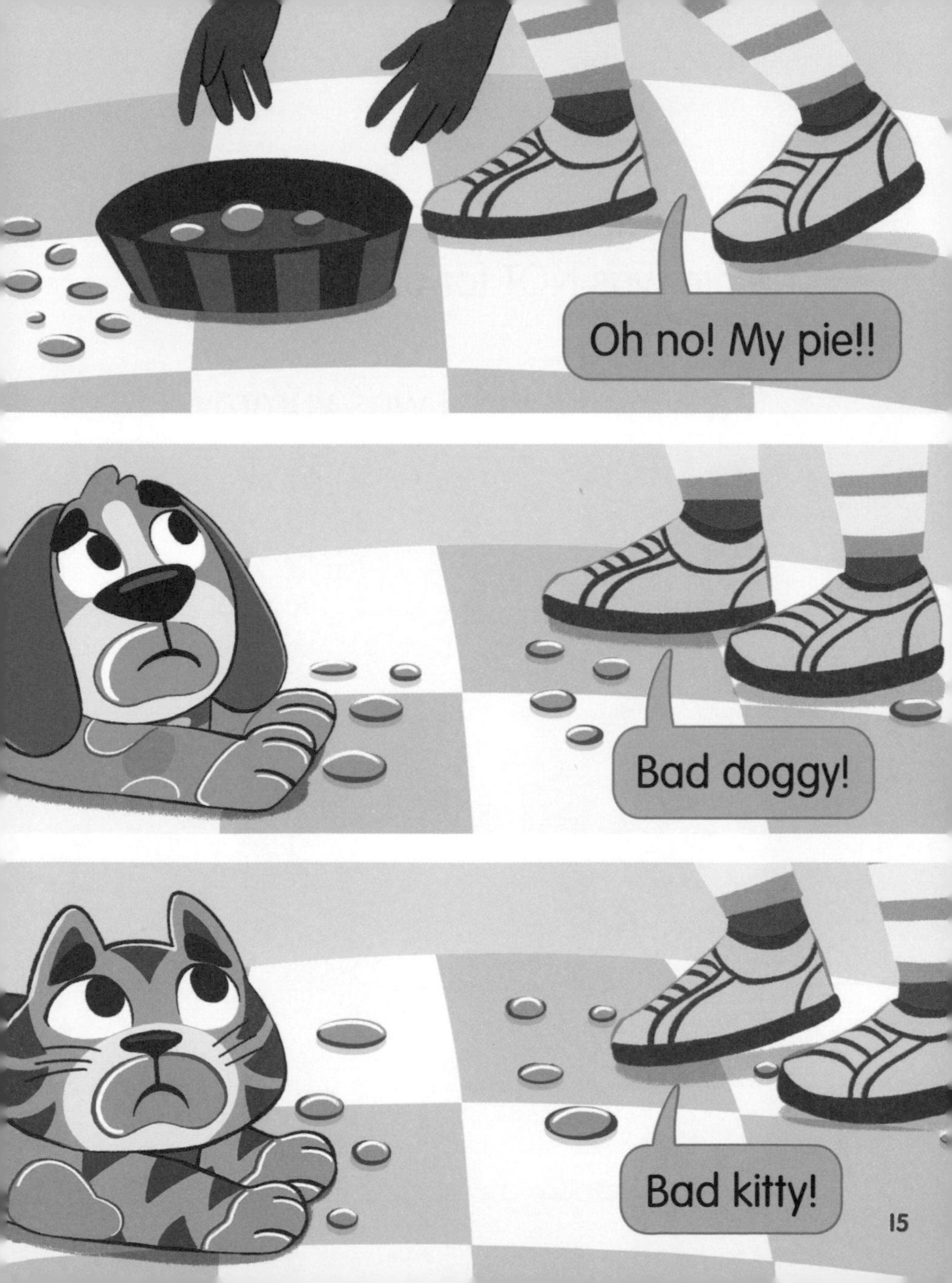
Oh no! My pie!!
Bad doggy!
Bad kitty!

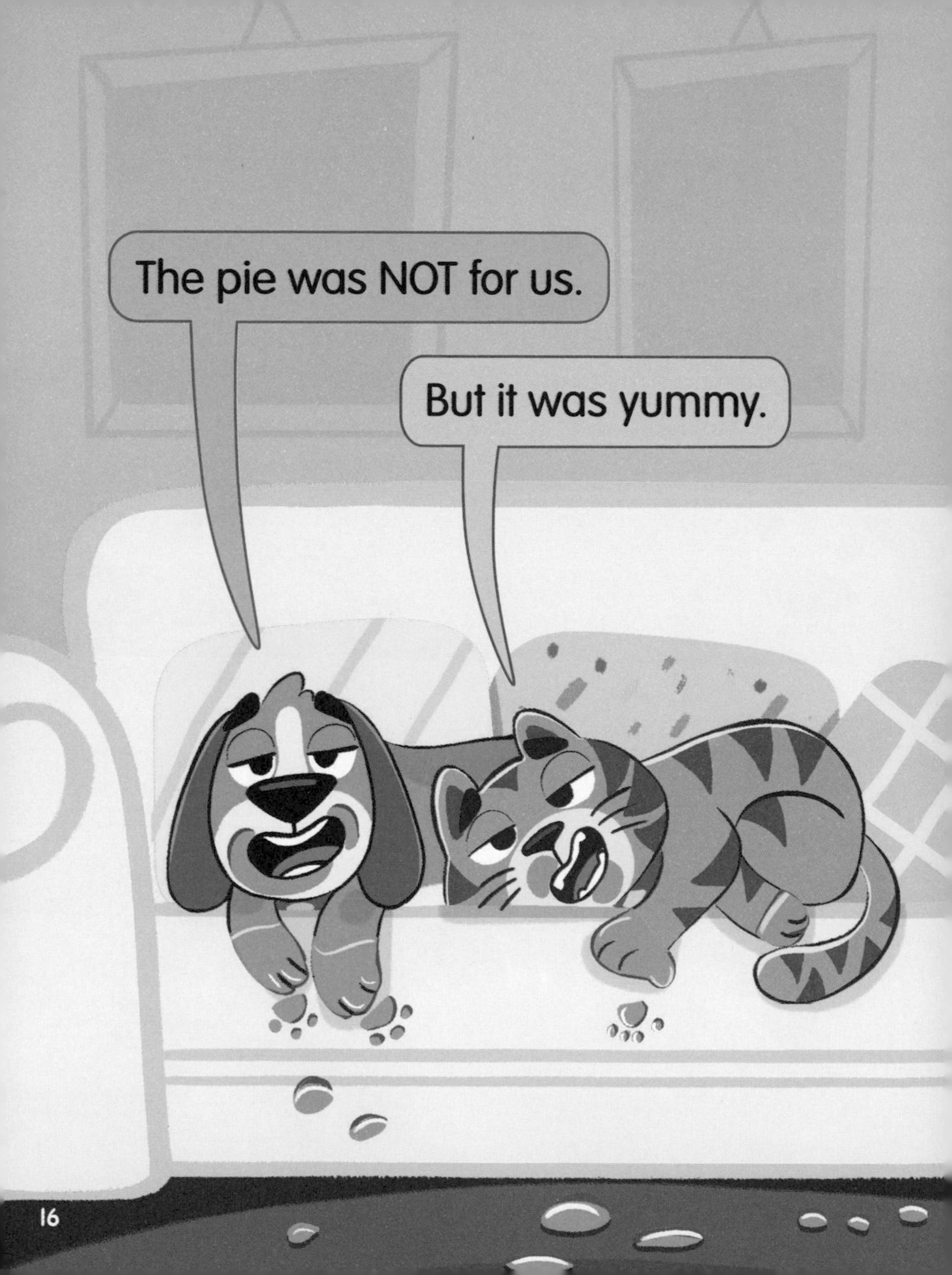
The pie was NOT for us.
But it was yummy.

The Box

A box is here.

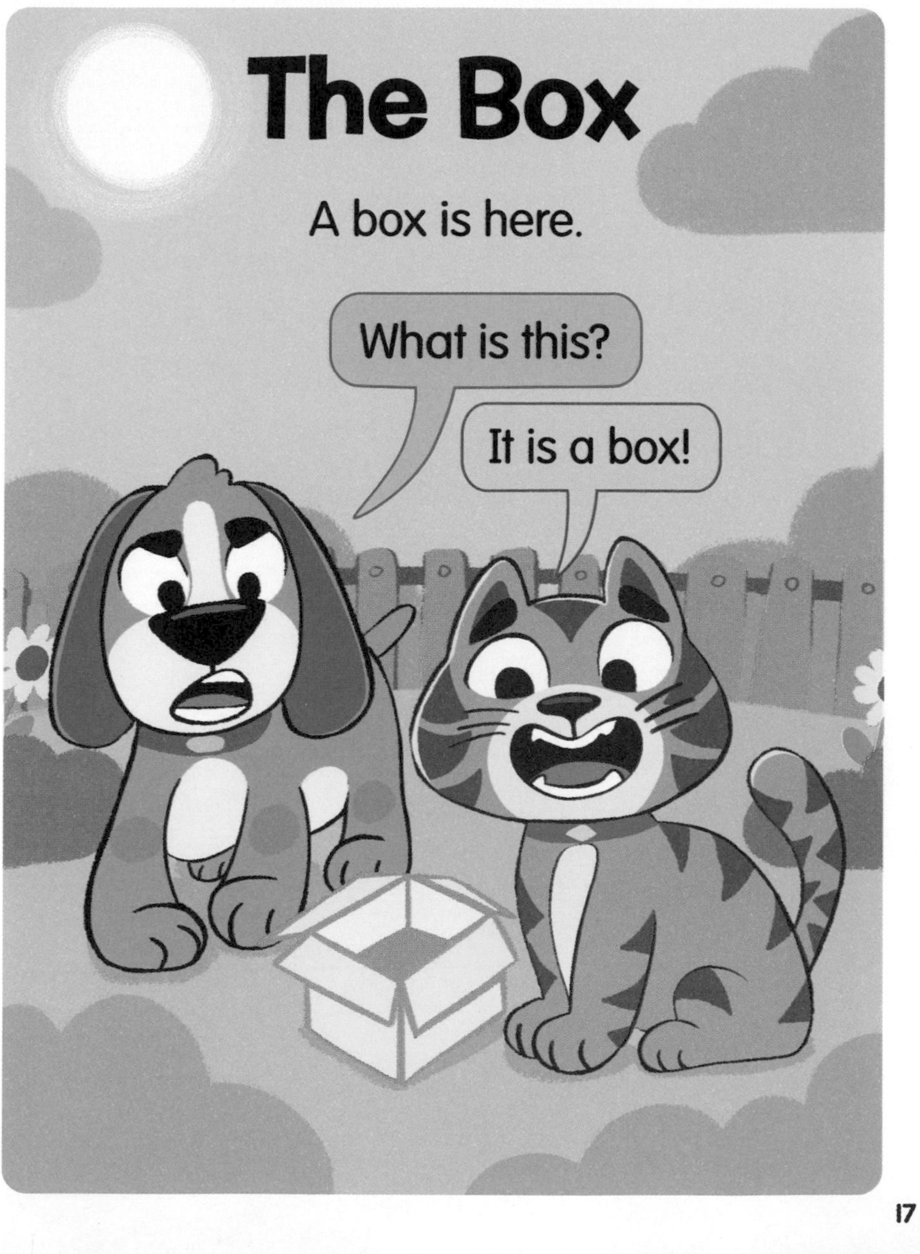
What is this?
It is a box!

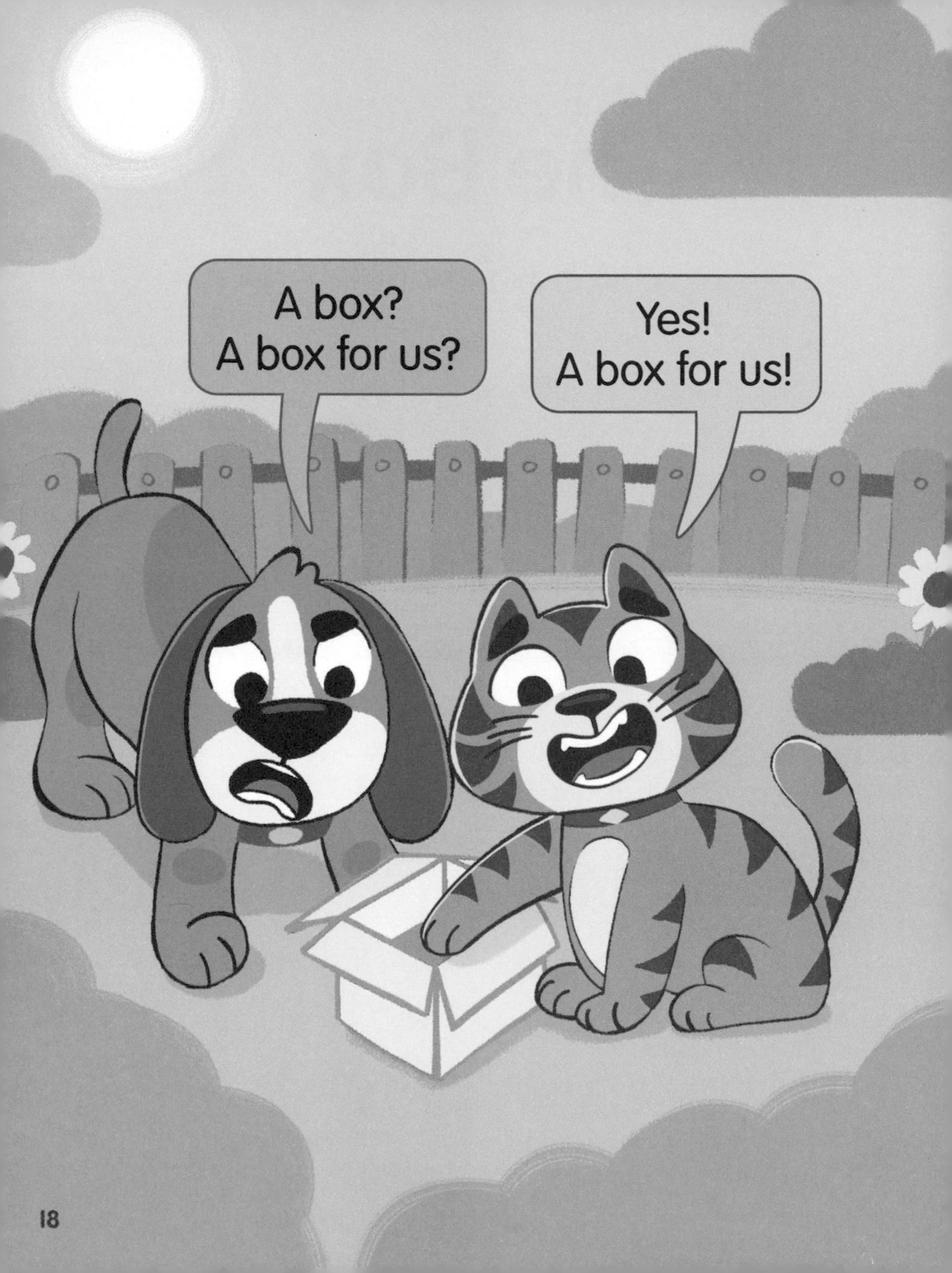
A box?
A box for us?
Yes!
A box for us!

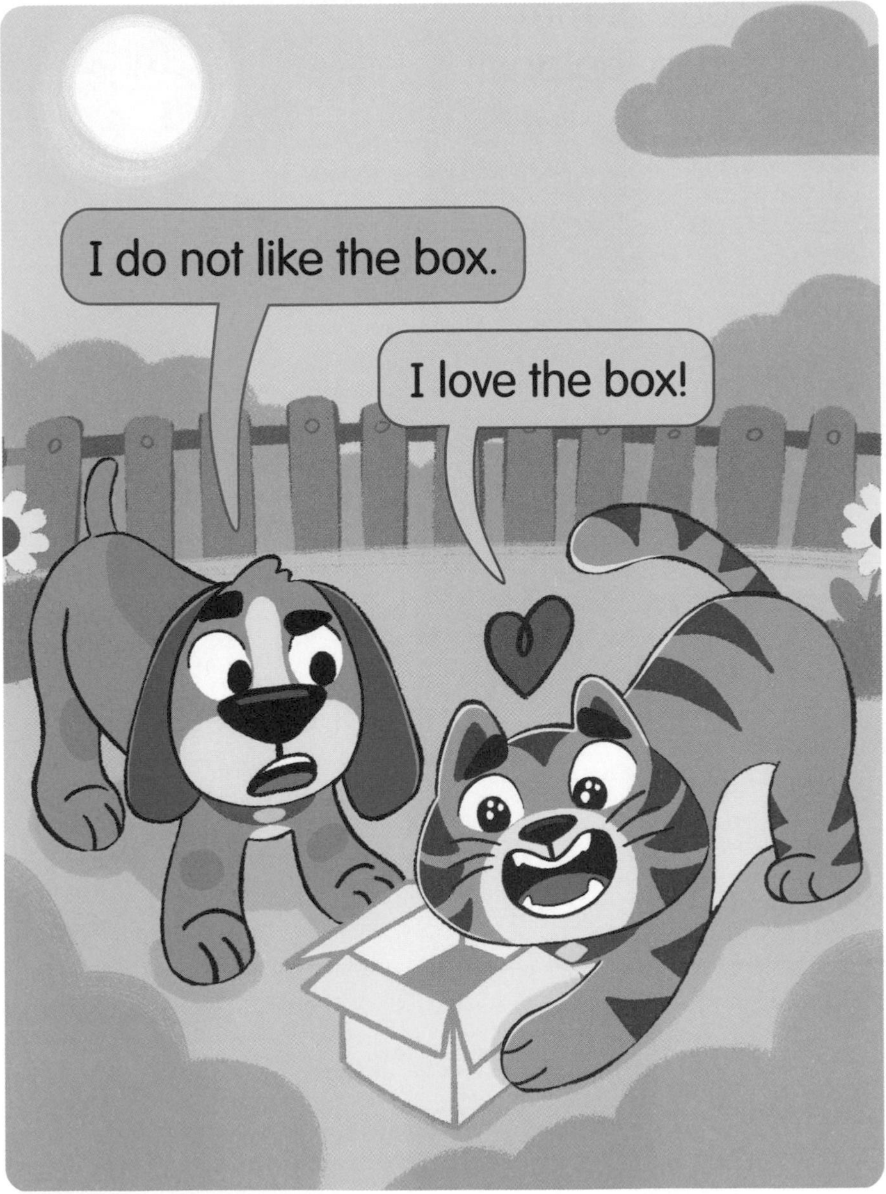
I do not like the box.
I love the box!

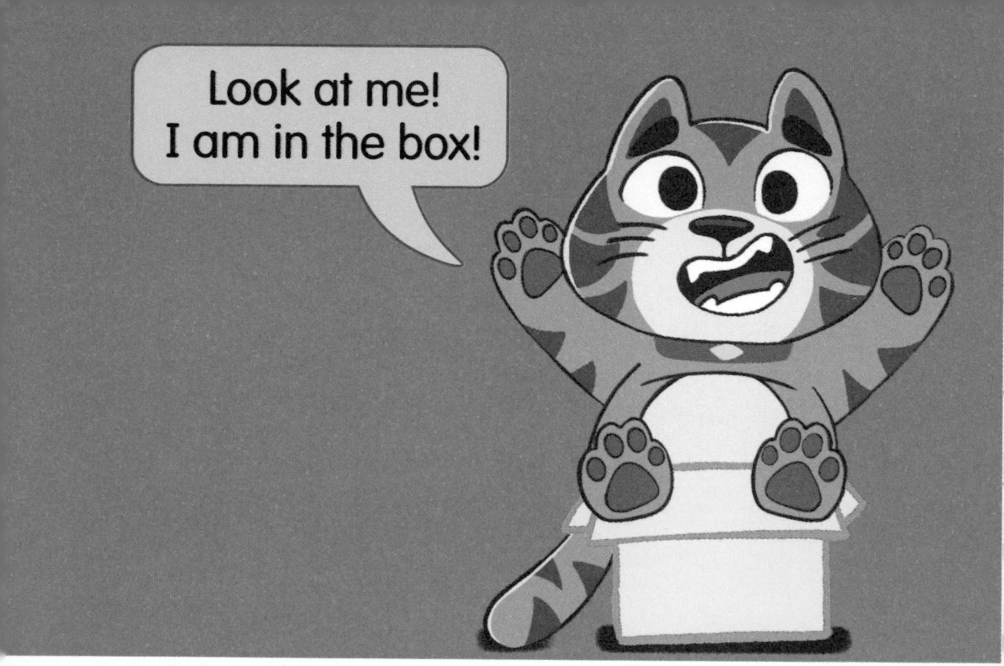
Look at me!
I am in the box!

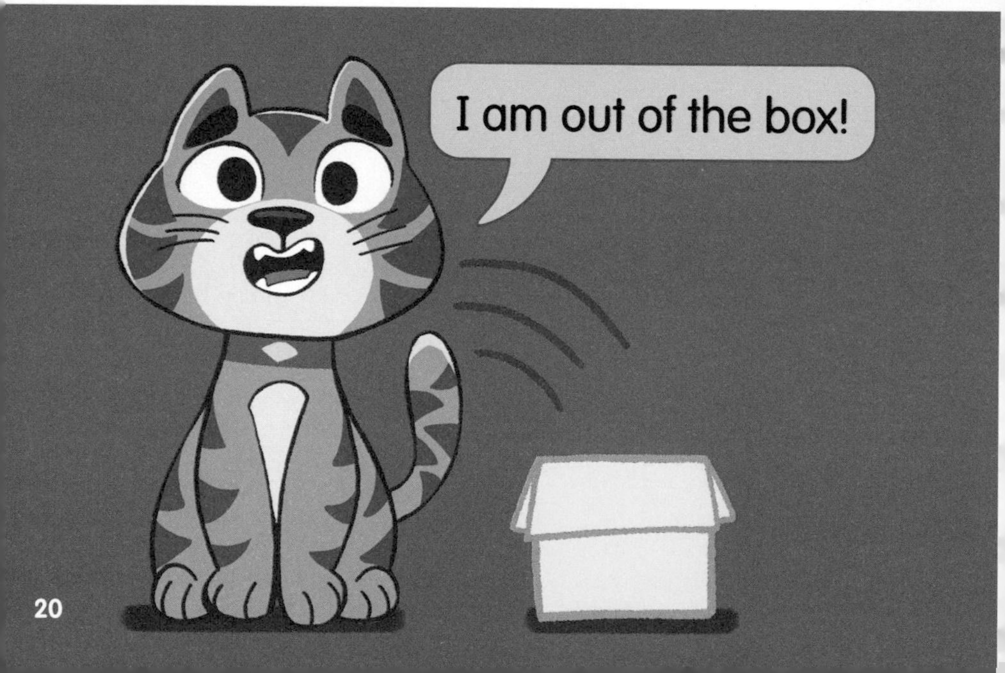
I am out of the box!

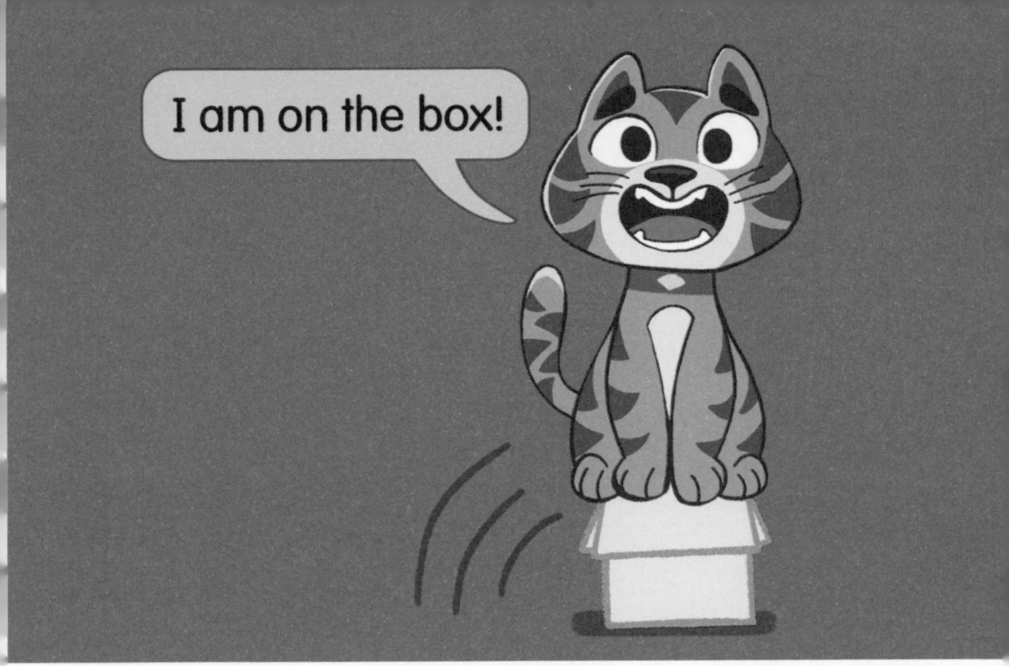
I am on the box!

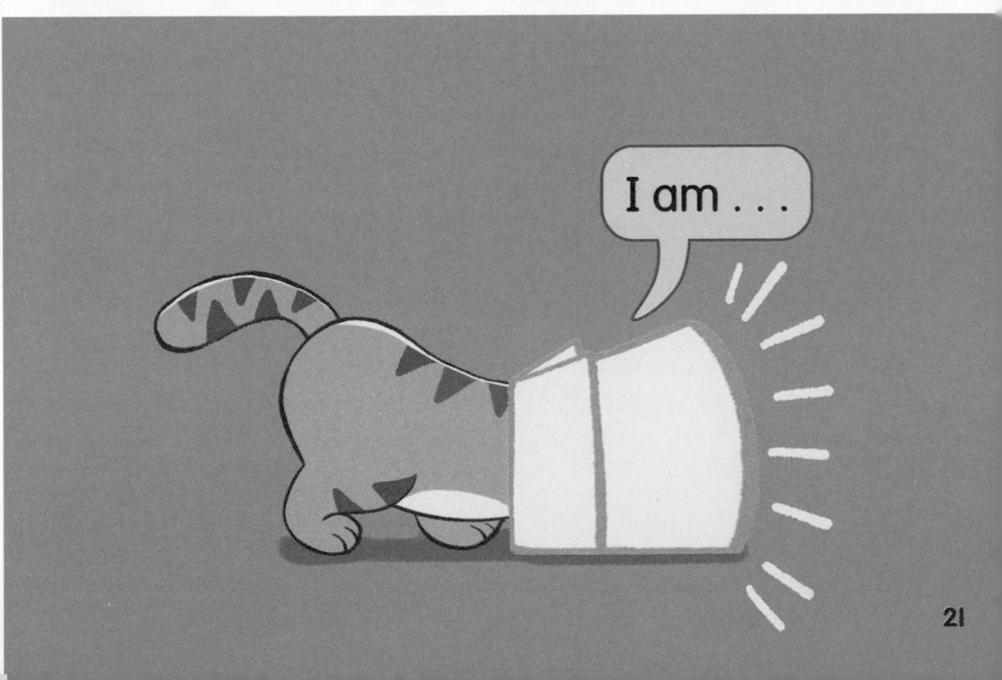
I am . . .

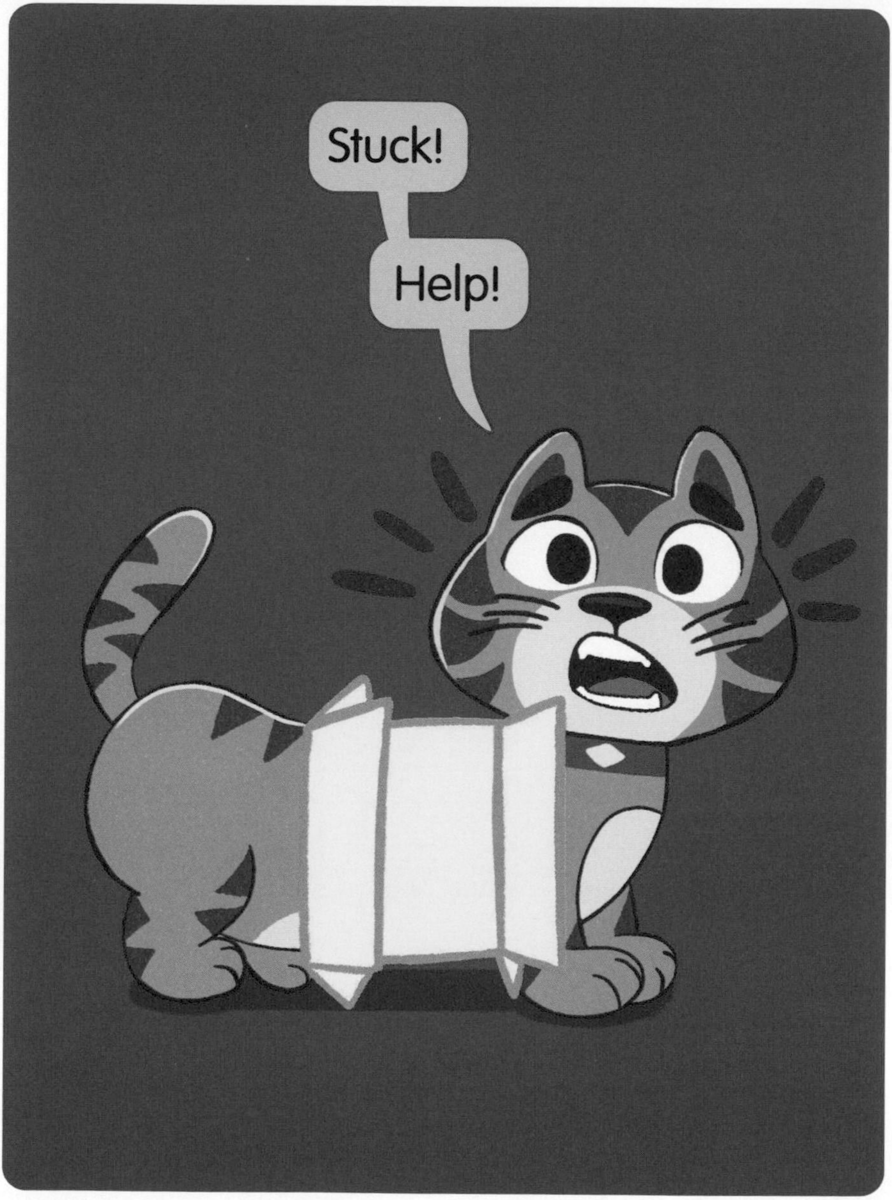
Stuck!
Help!

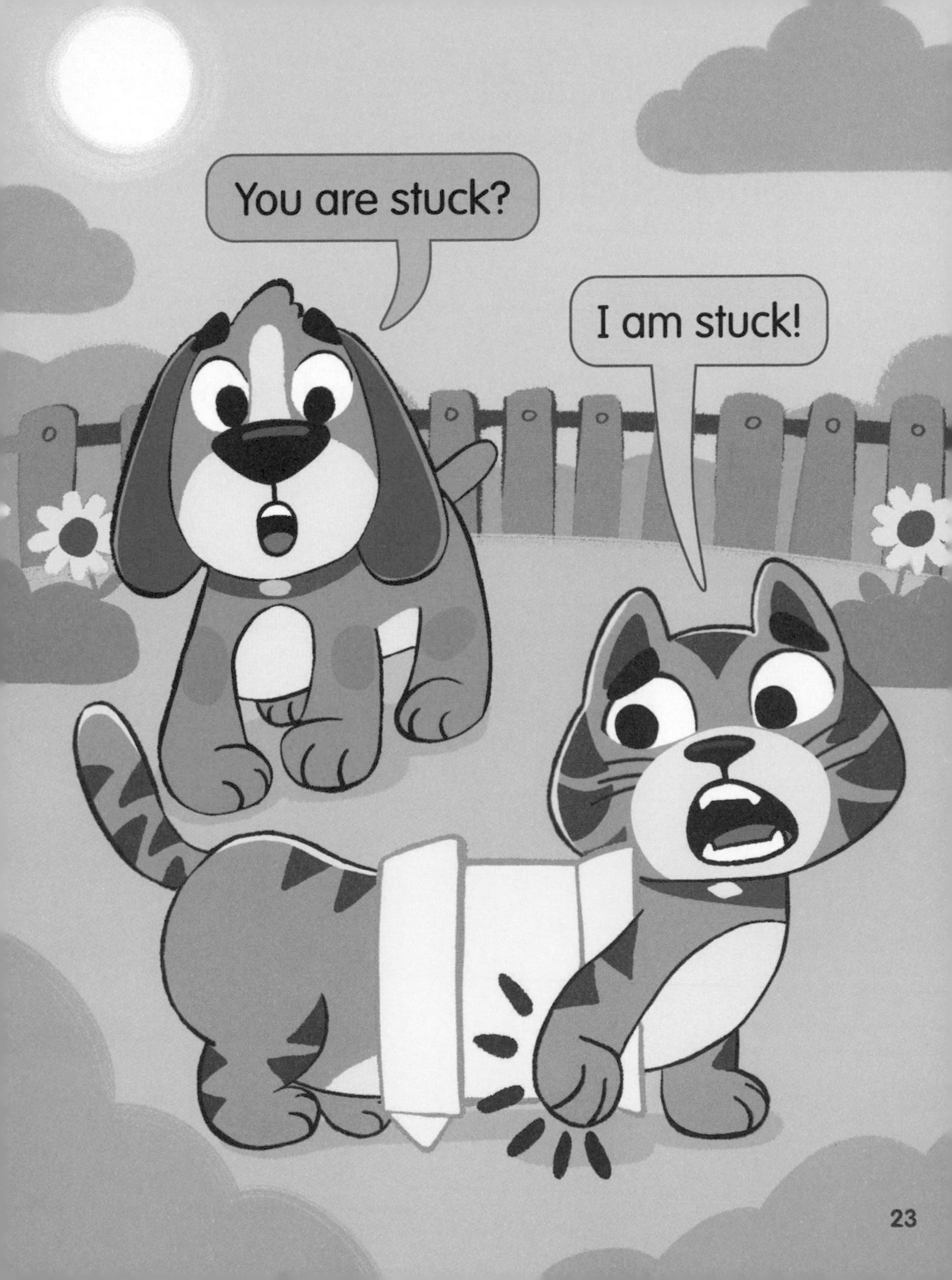
You are stuck?
I am stuck!

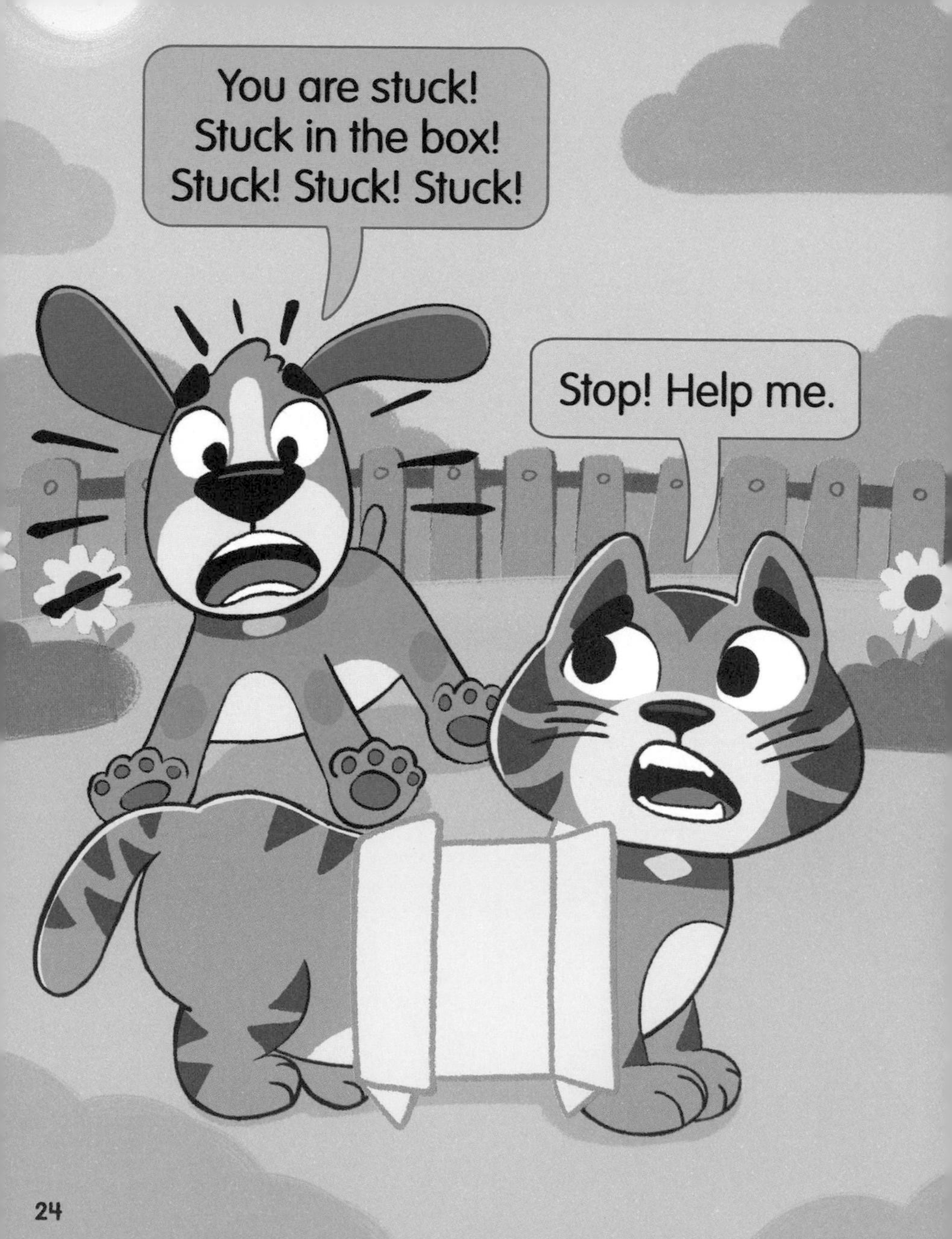
You are stuck!
Stuck in the box!
Stuck! Stuck! Stuck!
Stop! Help me.

Sniff sniffs.

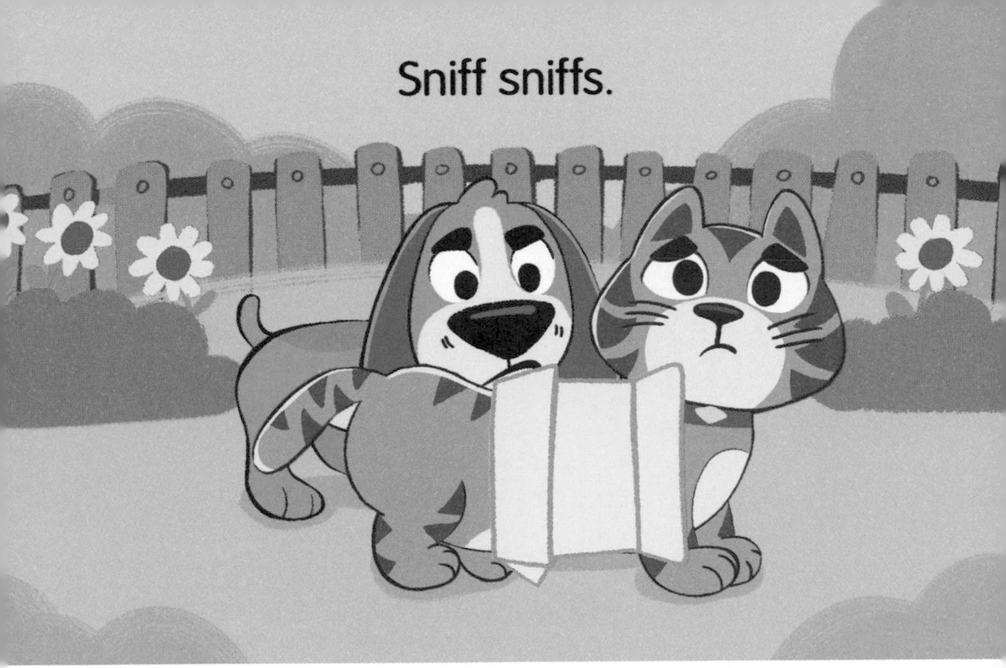

Scratch scratches.

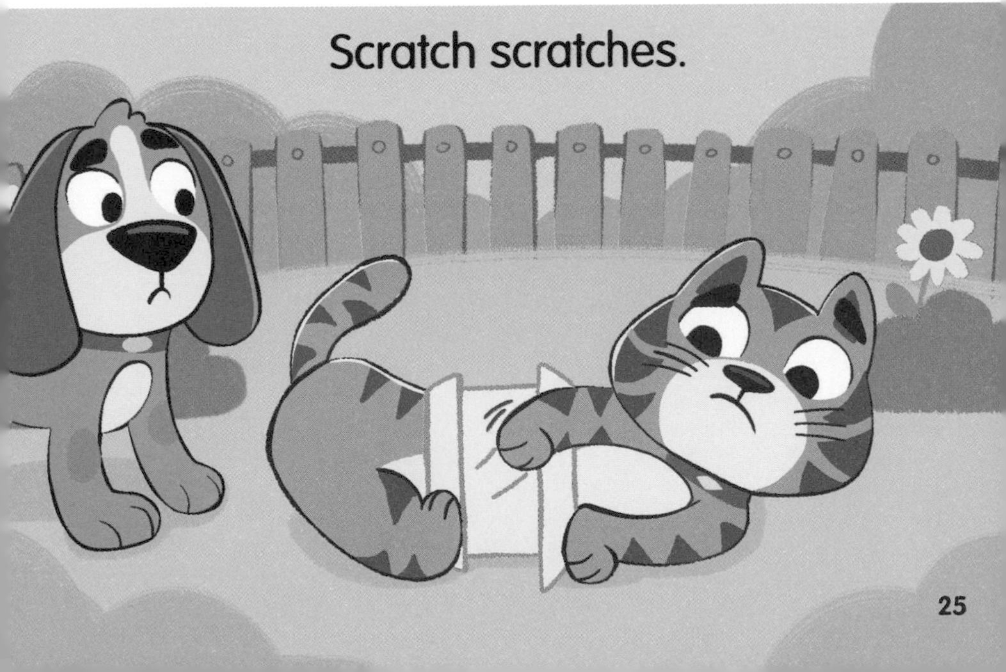

Sniff barks.

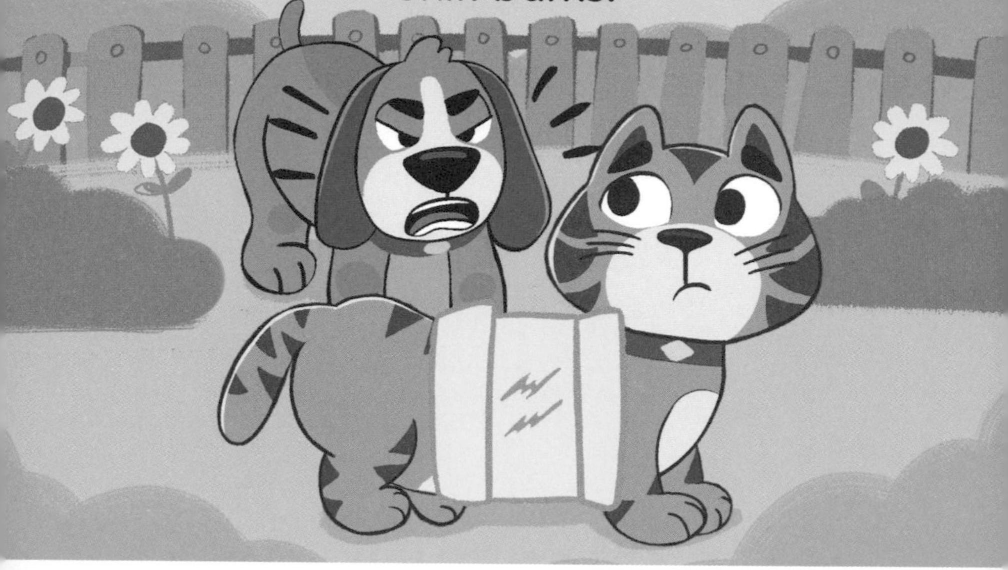

Scratch rolls.

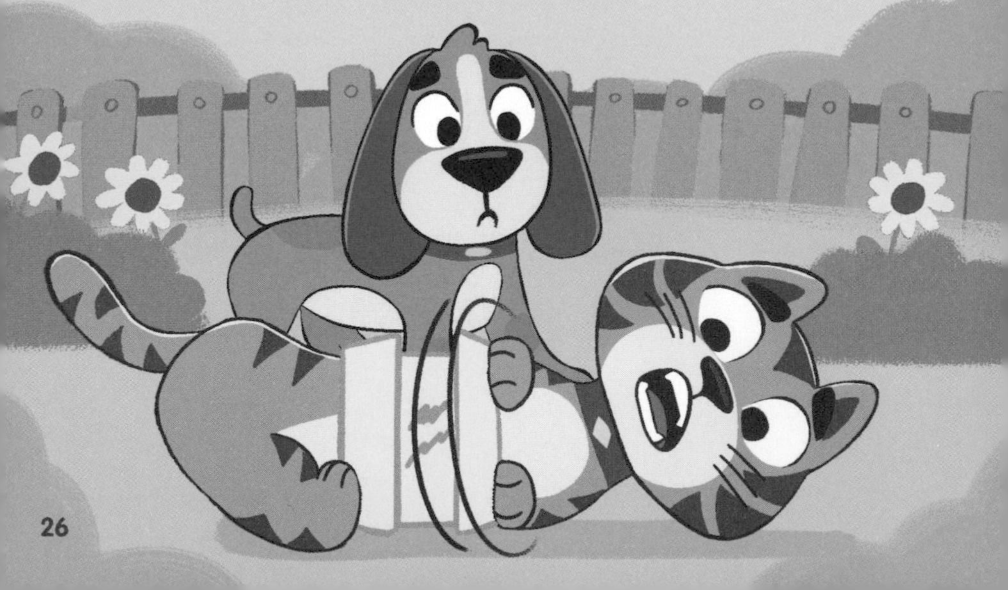

But the box does not move.

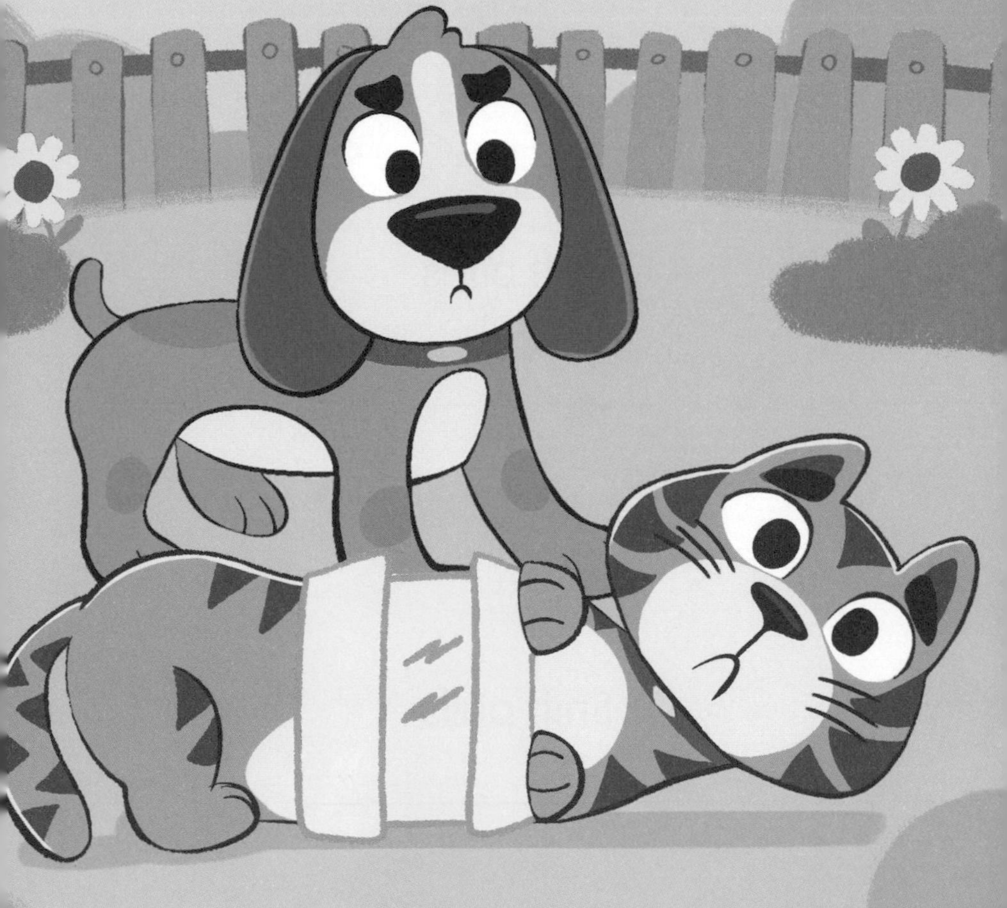

Scratch is stuck.

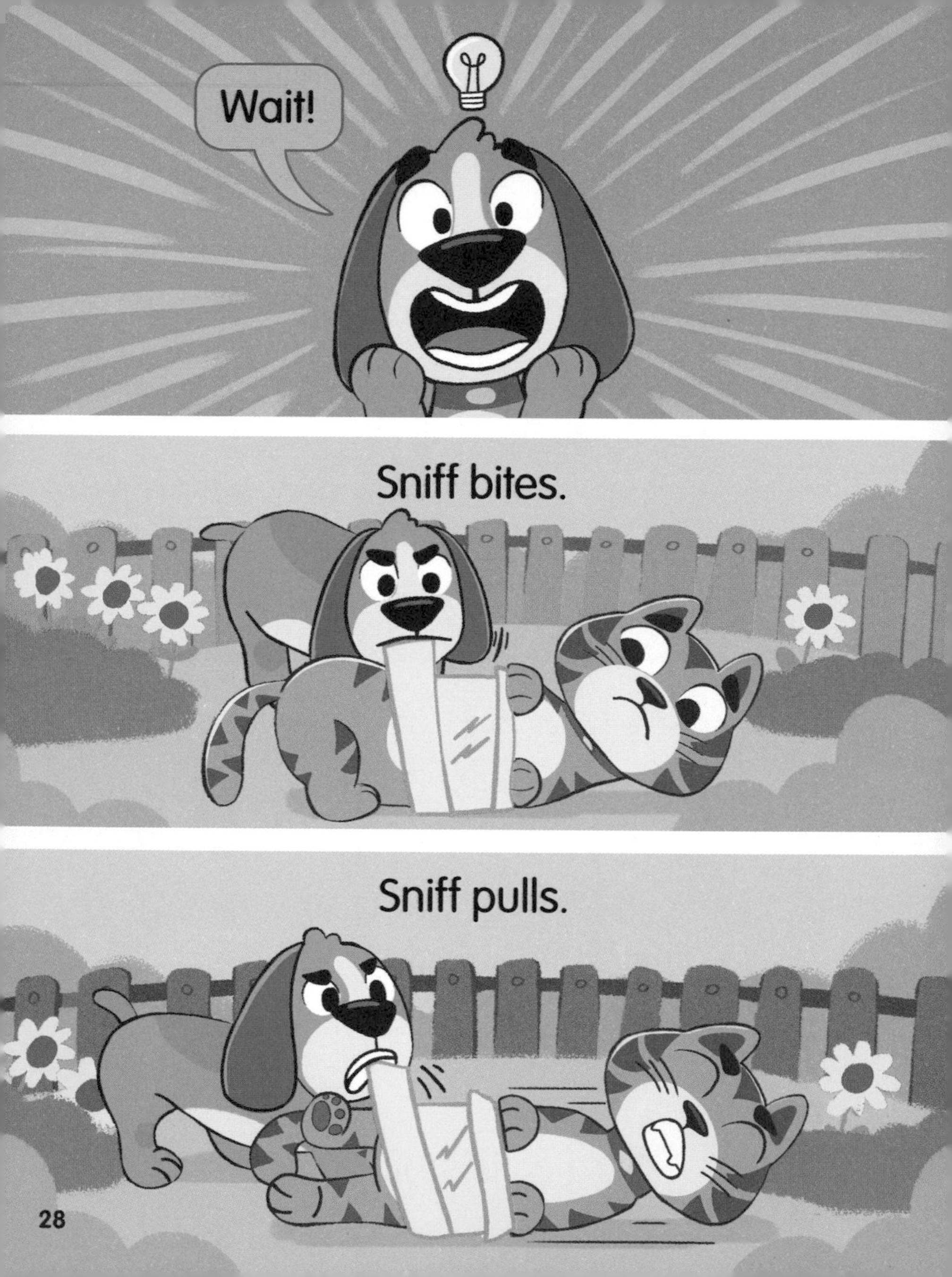
Wait!
Sniff bites.
Sniff pulls.

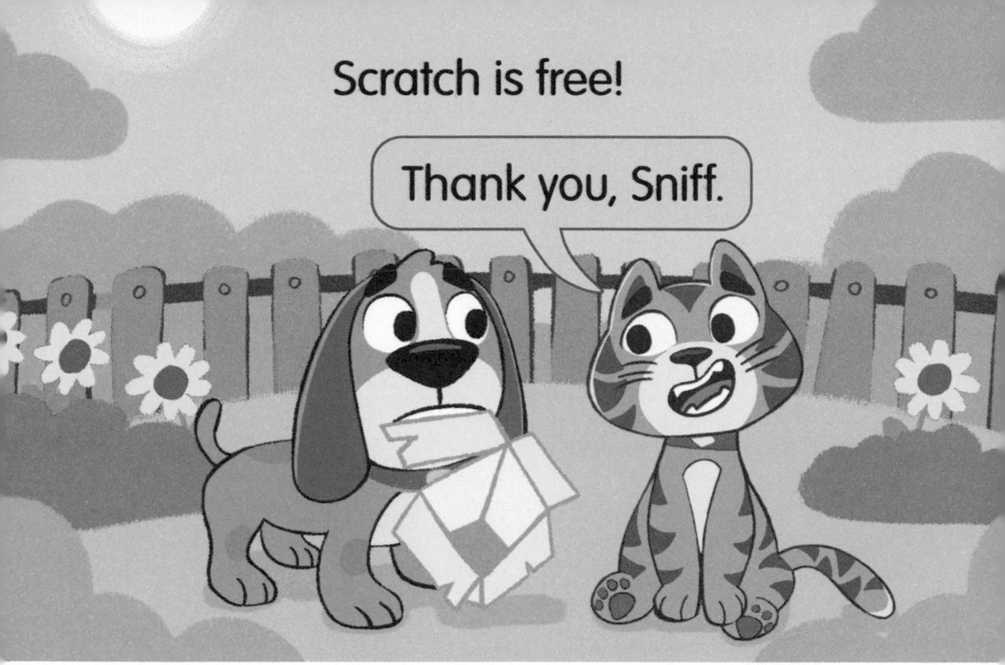
Scratch is free!
Thank you, Sniff.

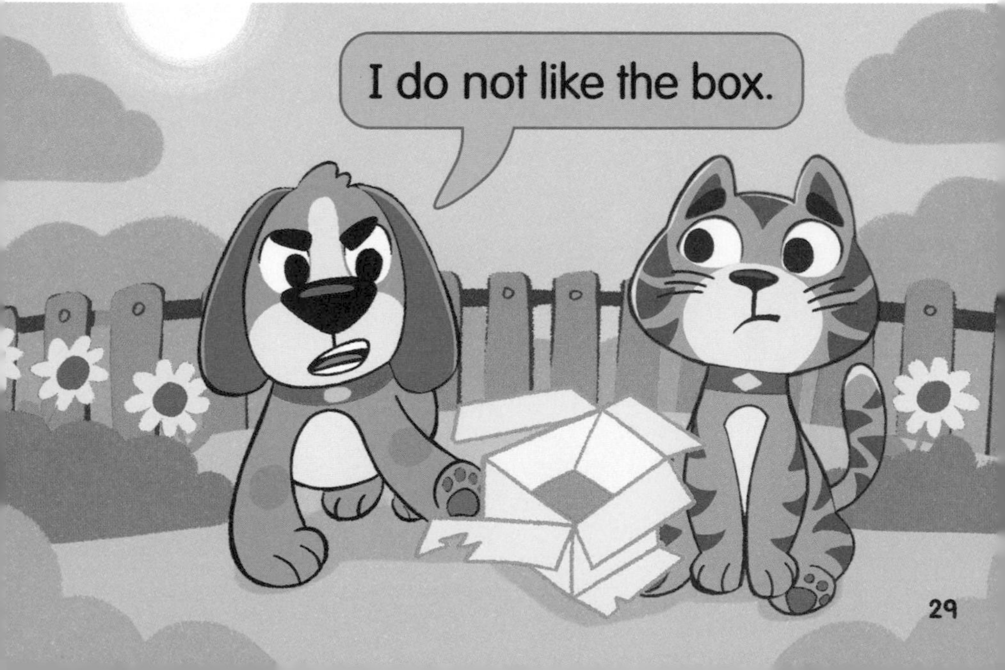
I do not like the box.

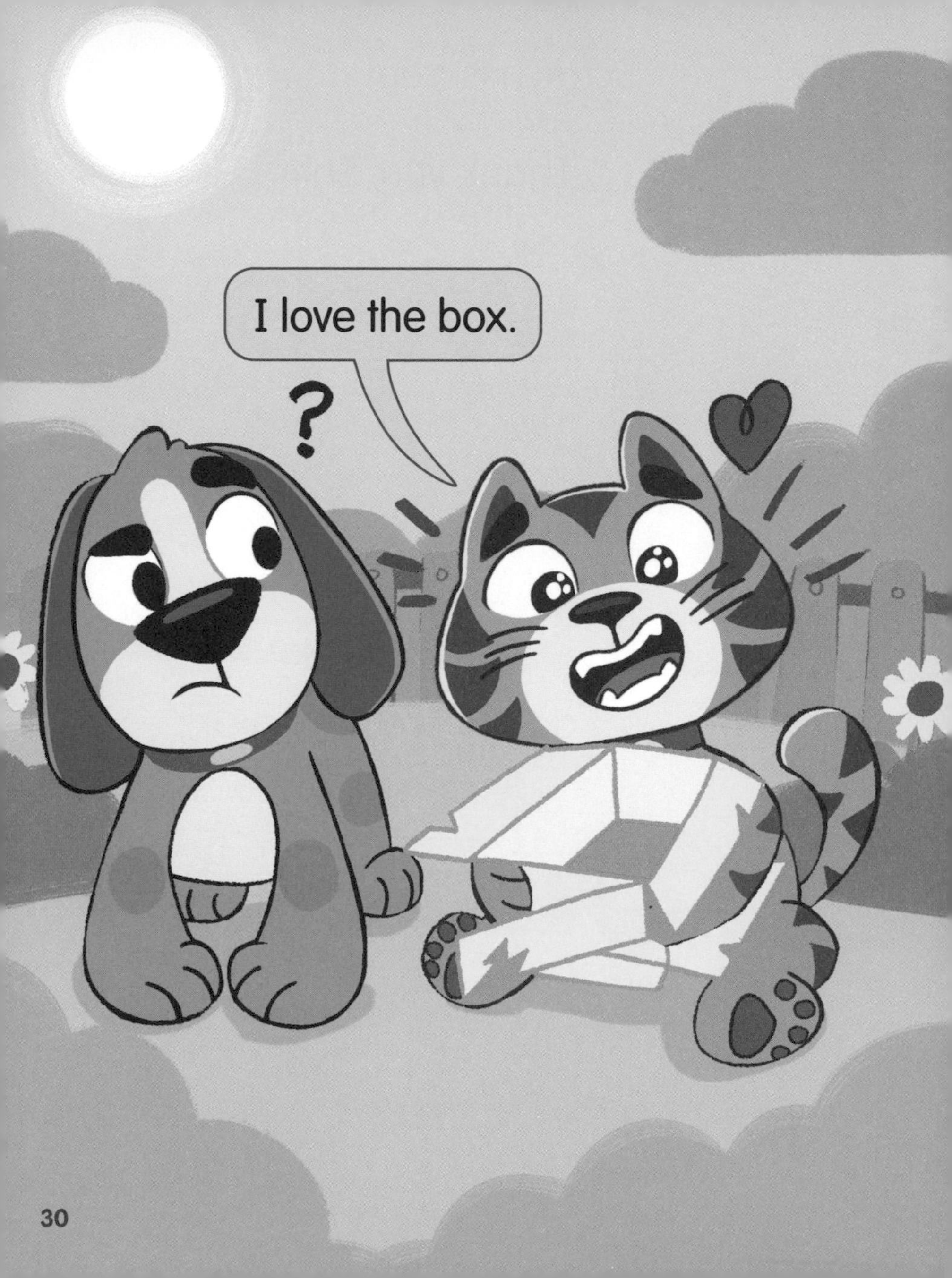
I love the box.
?

The Thing

A new thing is here.

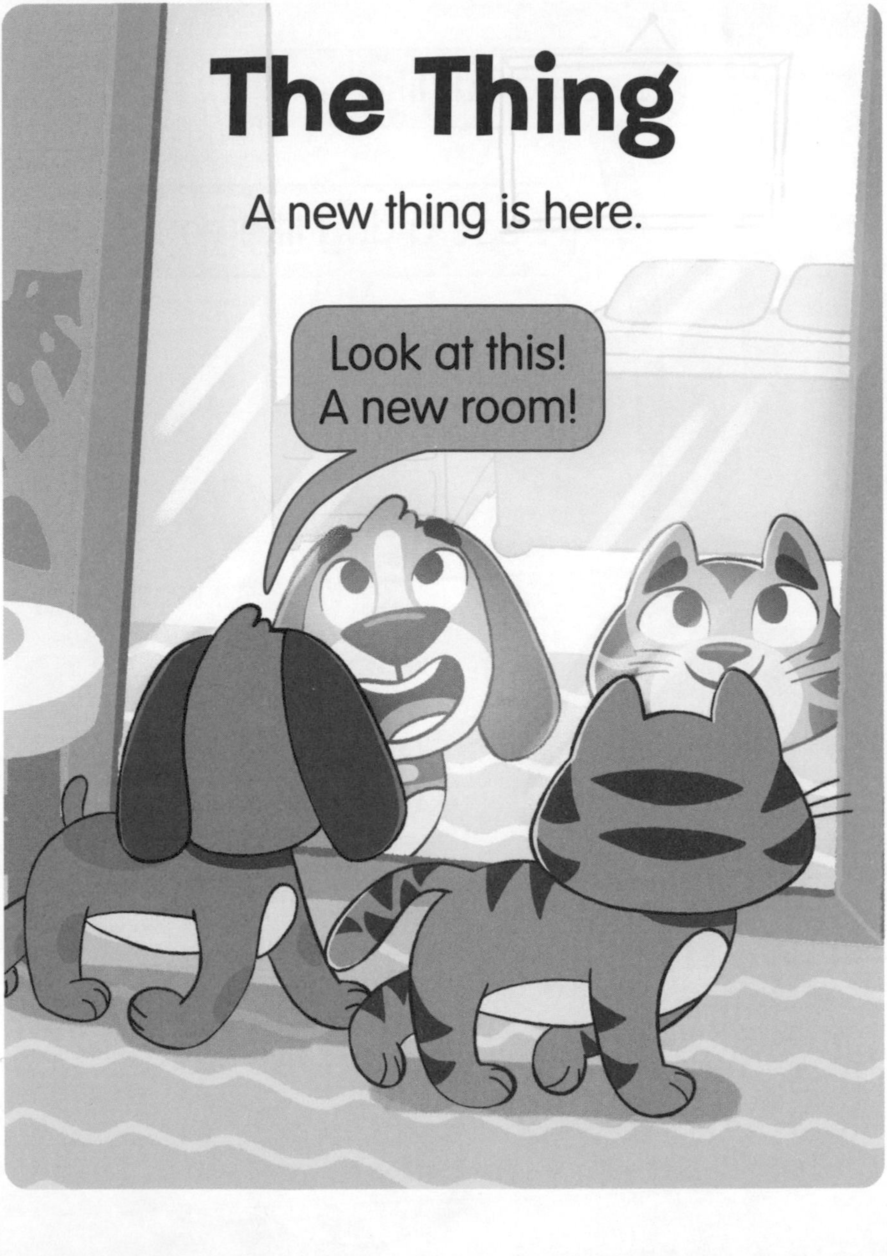
Look at this!
A new room!

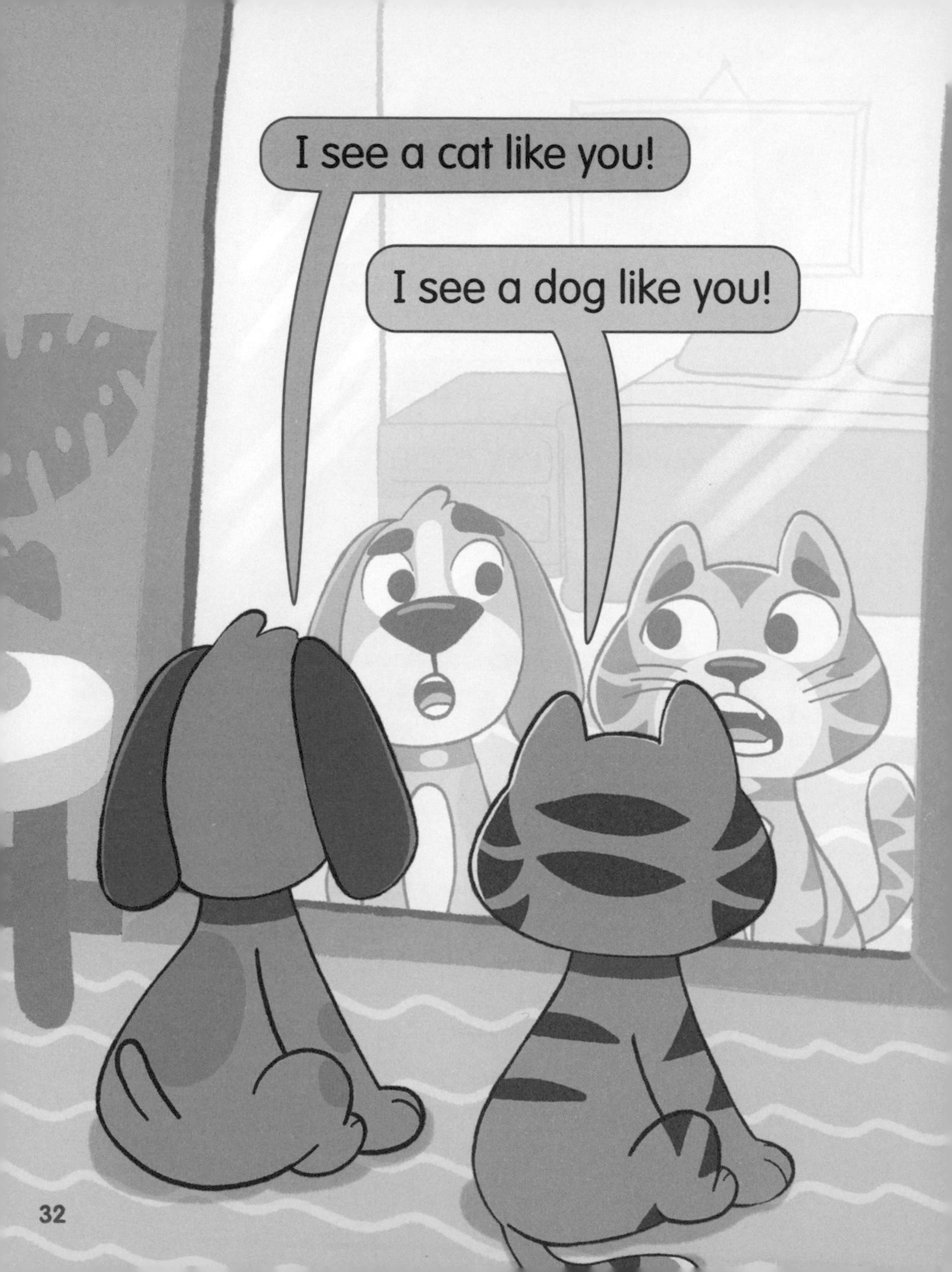
I see a cat like you!
I see a dog like you!

Sniff barks.

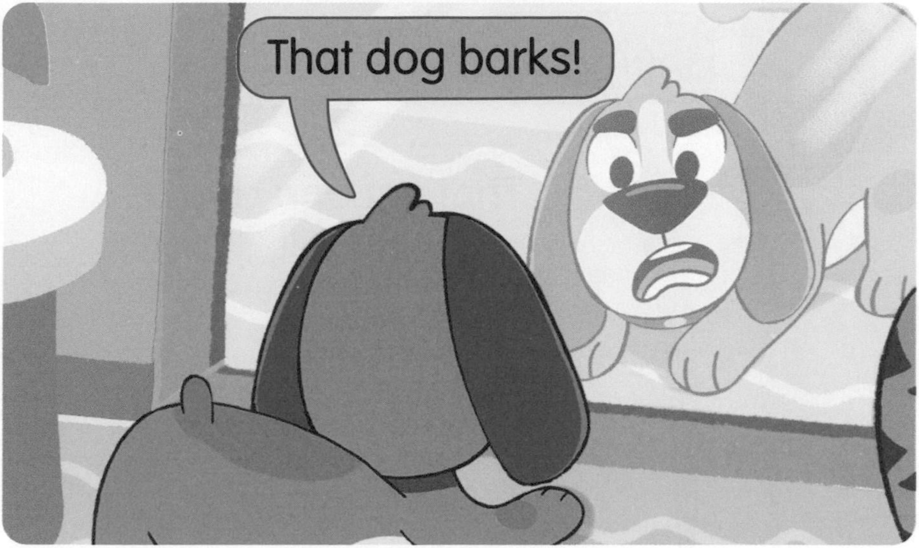
That dog barks!

Scratch hisses.

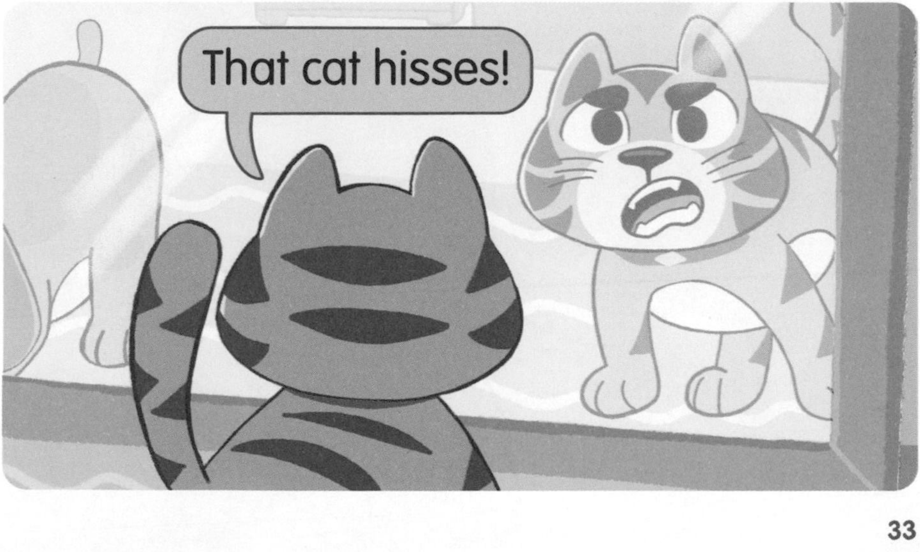
That cat hisses!

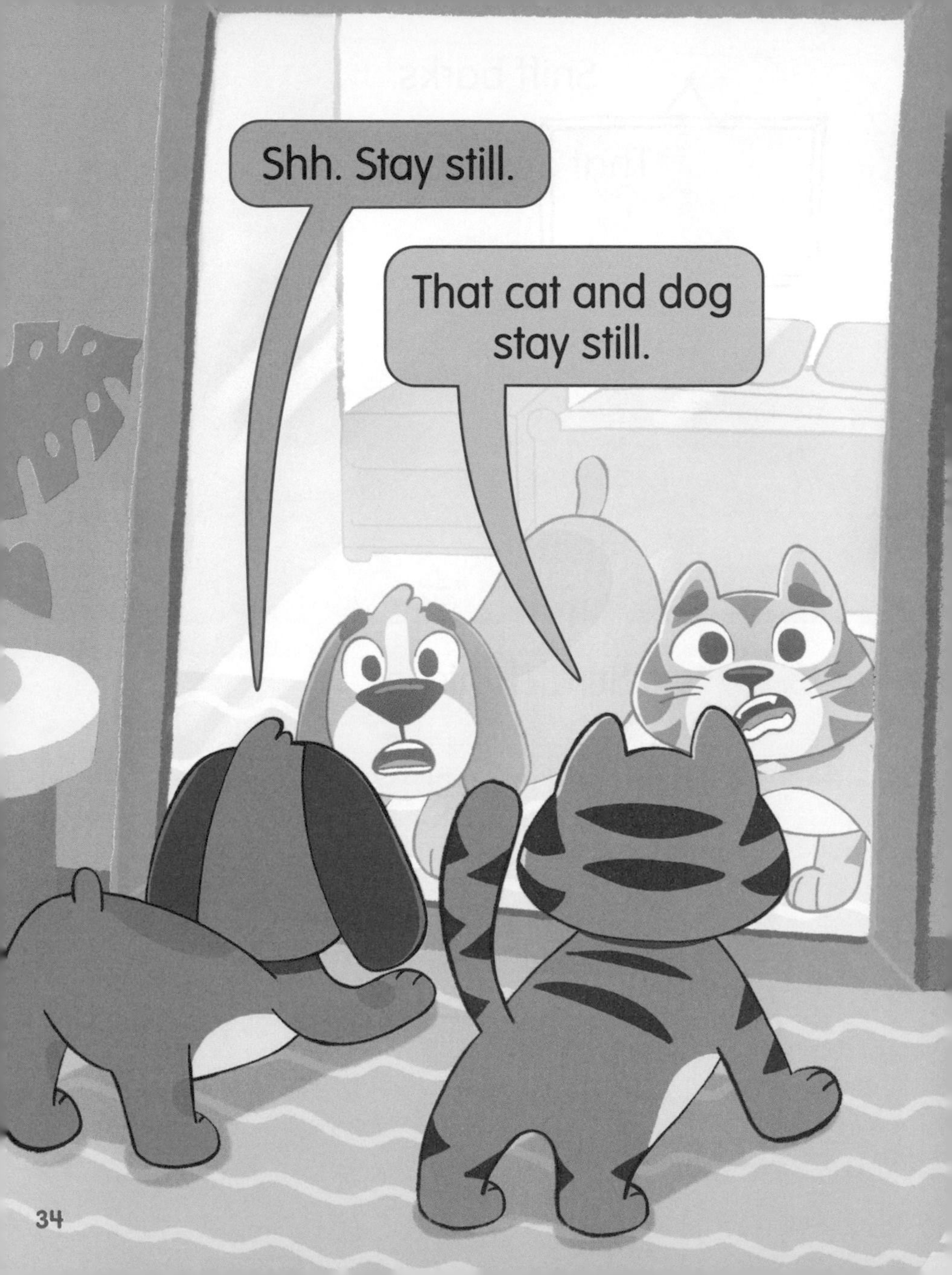
Shh. Stay still.
That cat and dog stay still.

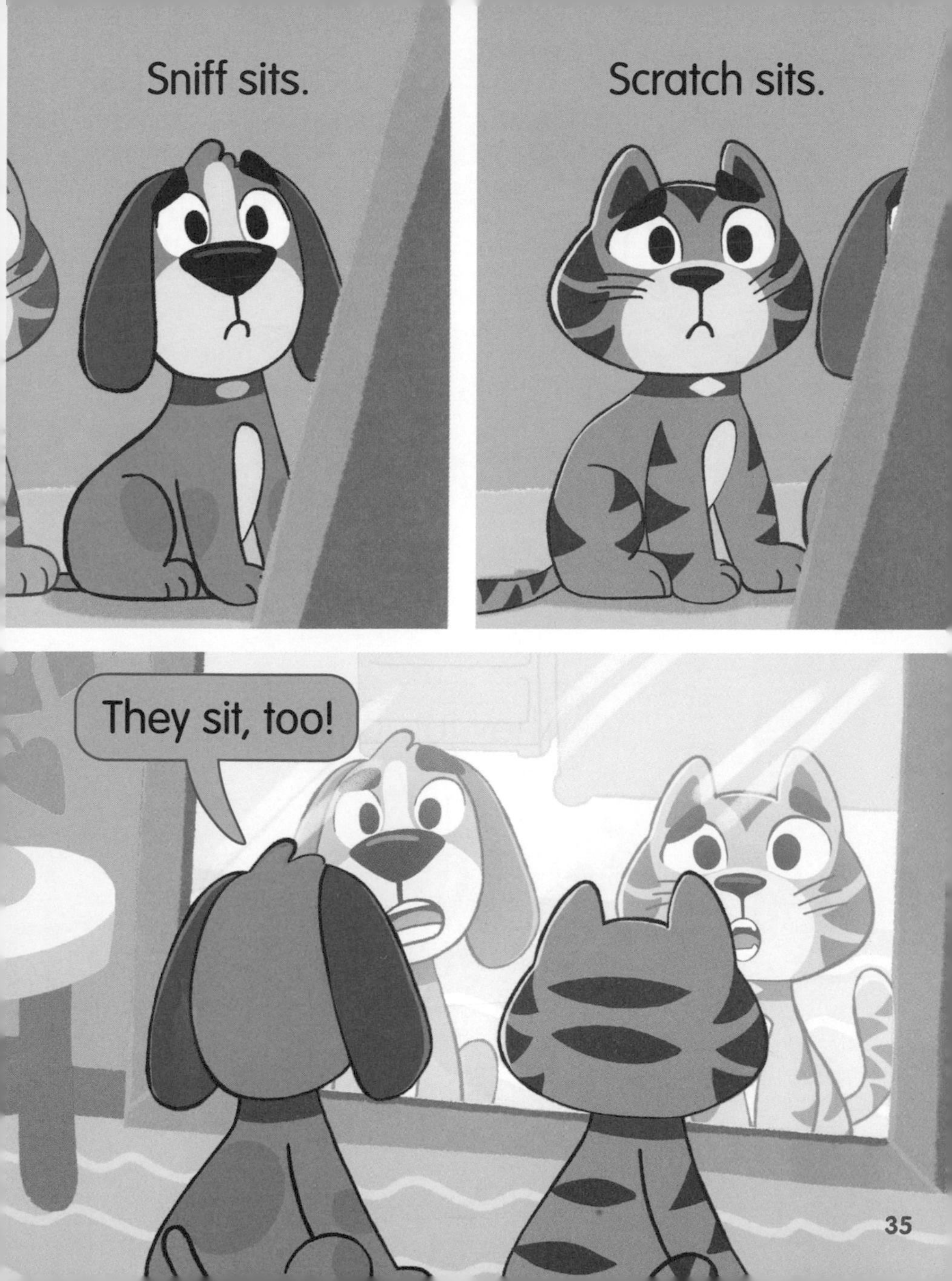
Sniff sits.
Scratch sits.
They sit, too!

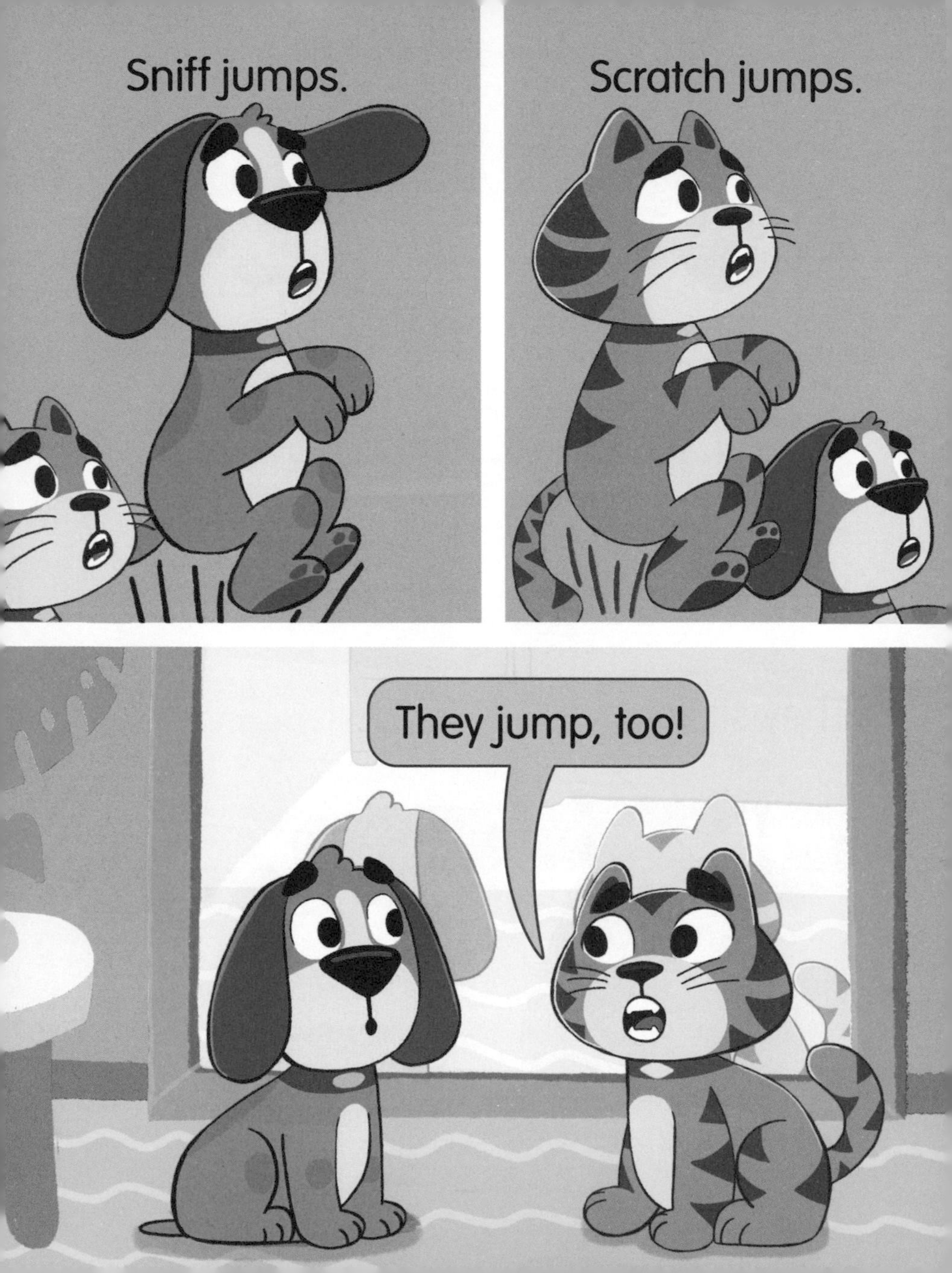
Sniff jumps.
Scratch jumps.
They jump, too!

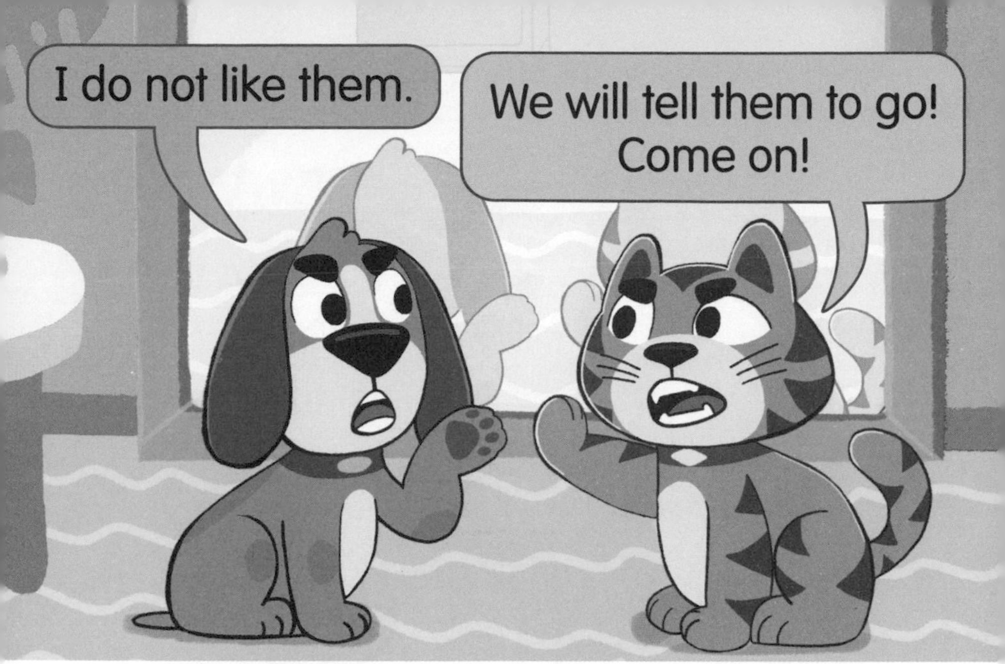
I do not like them.
We will tell them to go! Come on!

Sniff and Scratch try to run into the new room.

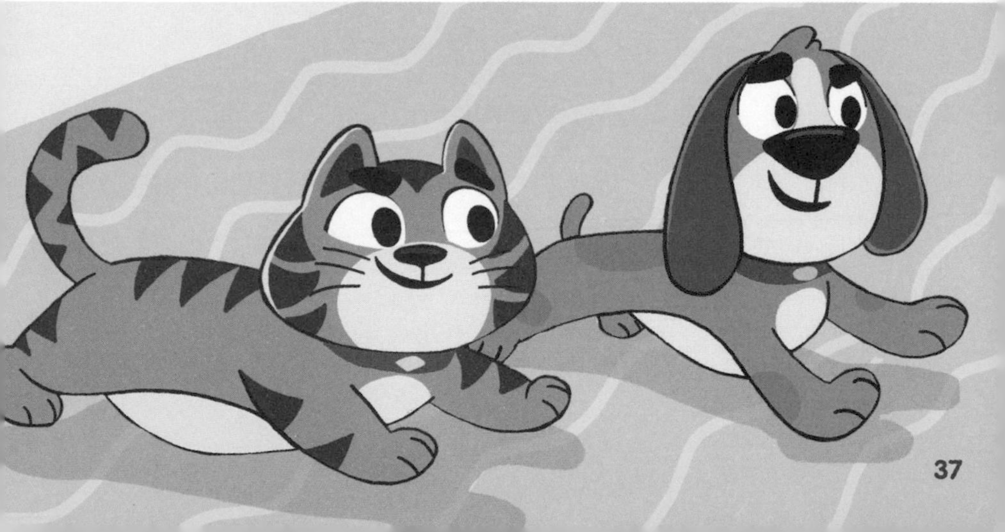

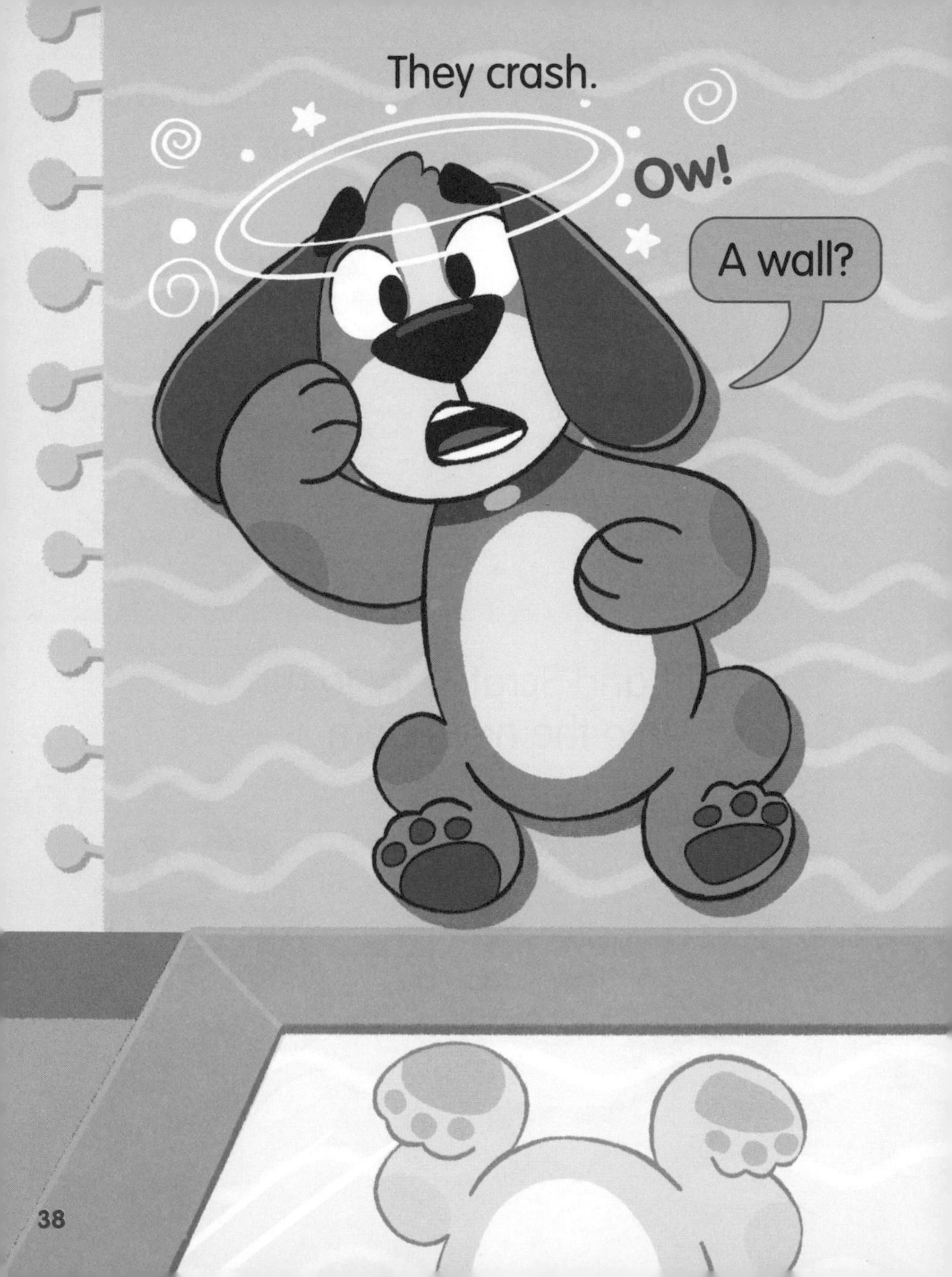
They crash.
Ow!
A wall?

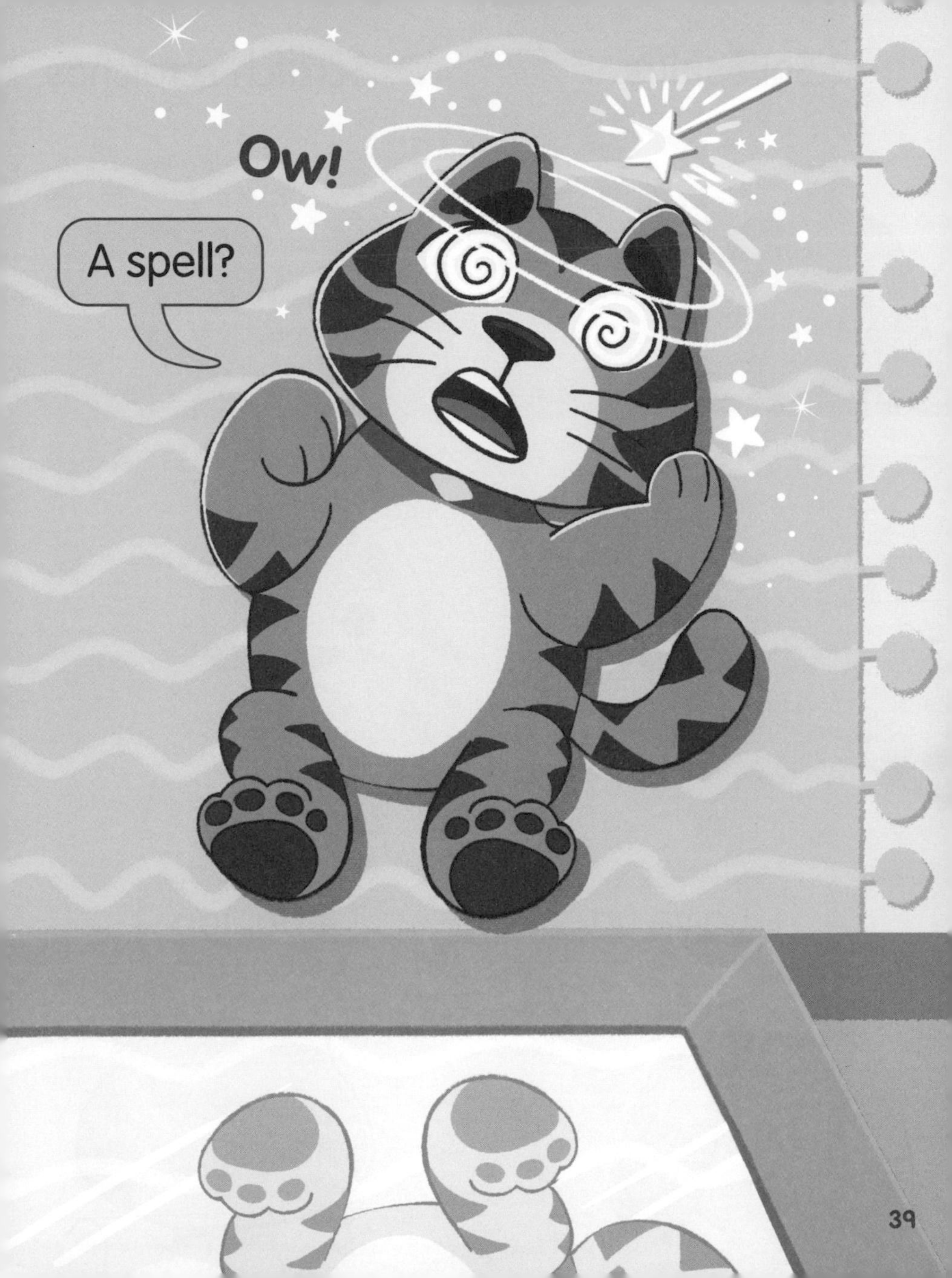
Ow!
A spell?

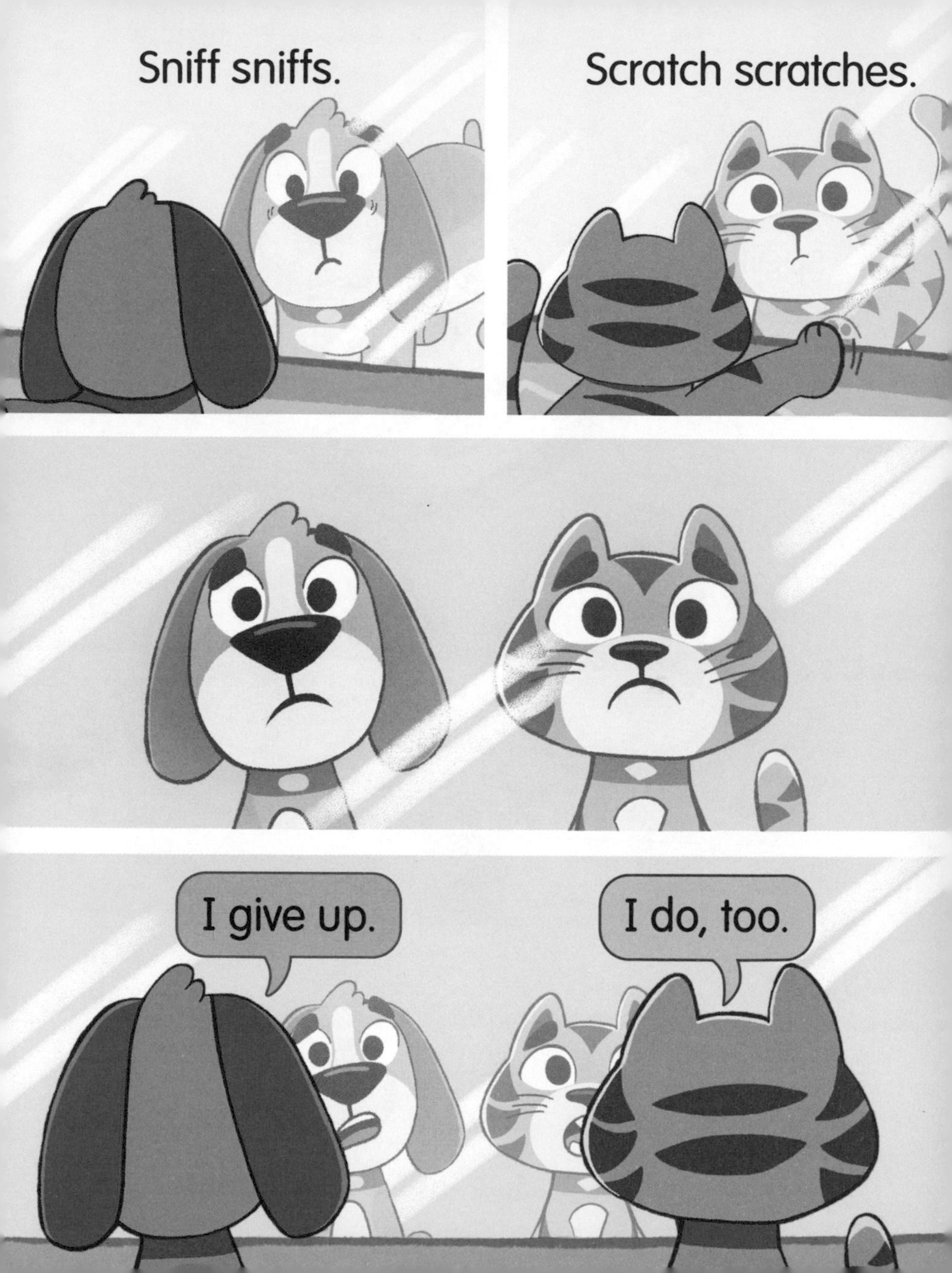
Sniff sniffs.
Scratch scratches.
I give up.
I do, too.

Sniff and Scratch back away.

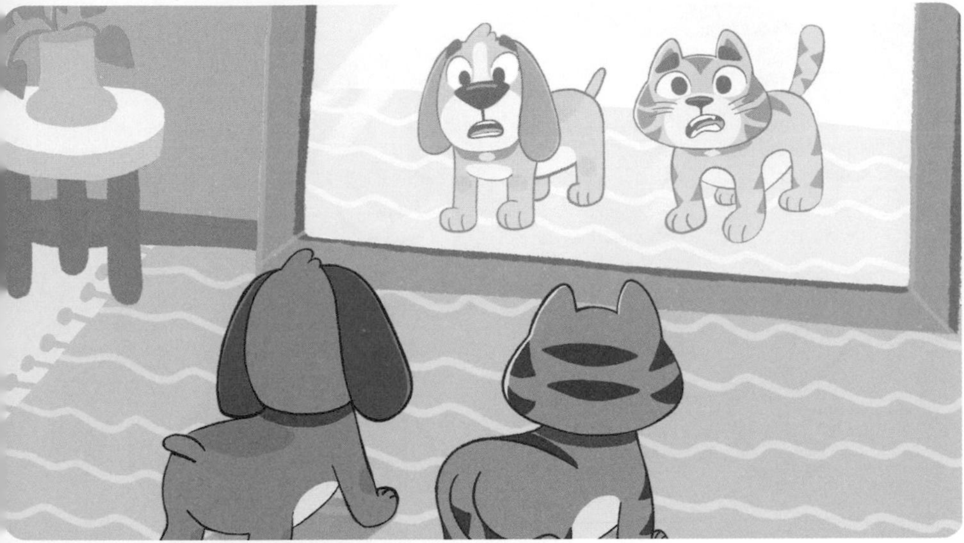

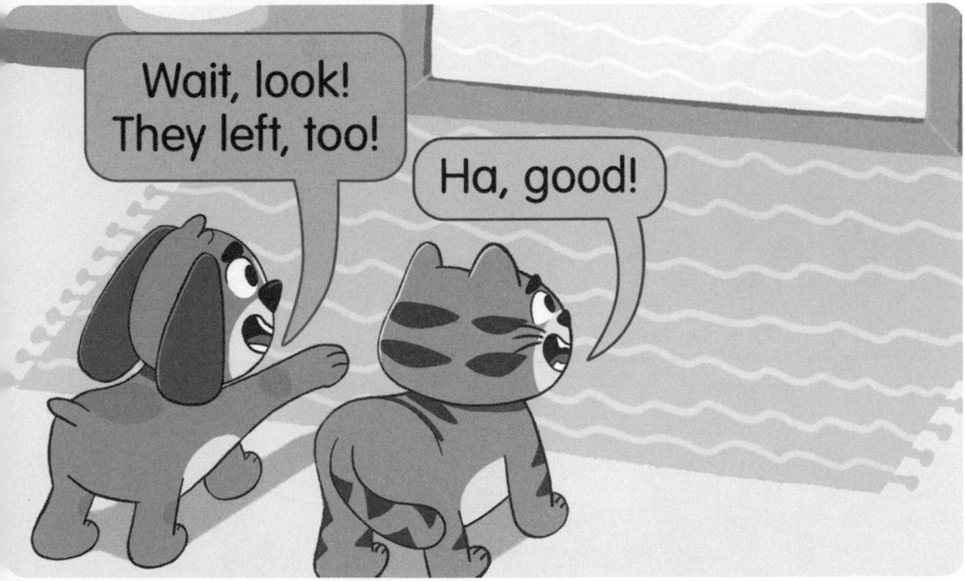
Wait, look! They left, too!
Ha, good!

Sniff and Scratch are happy.

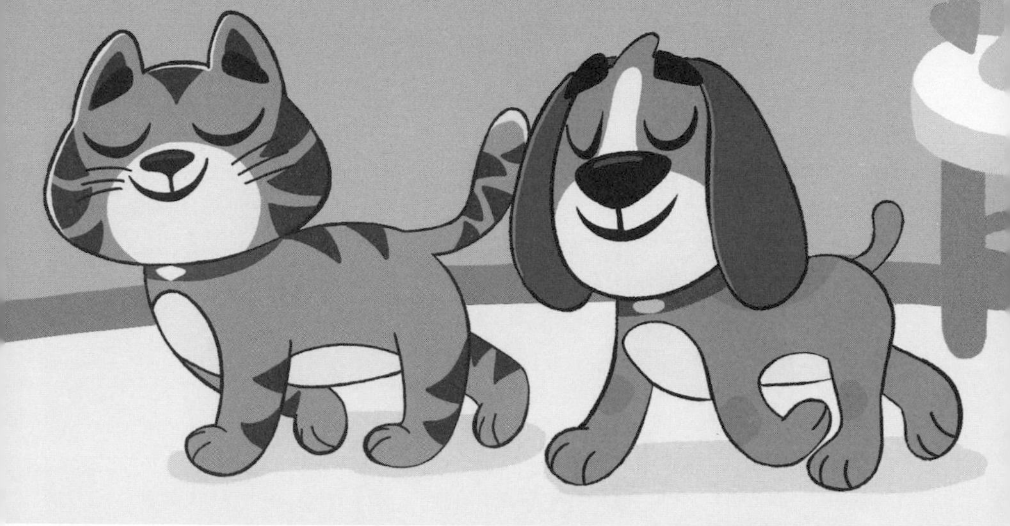

Well, mostly.

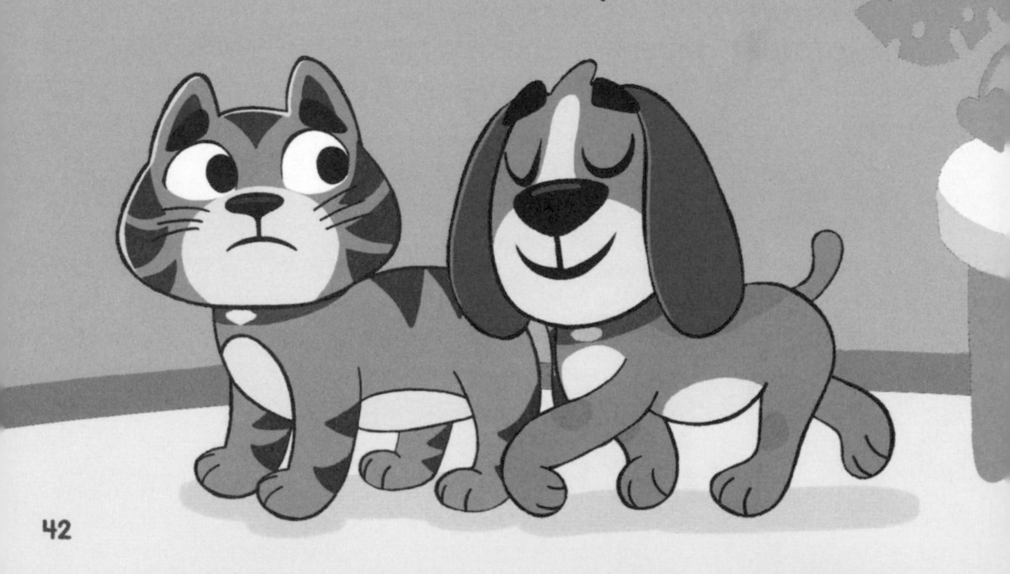

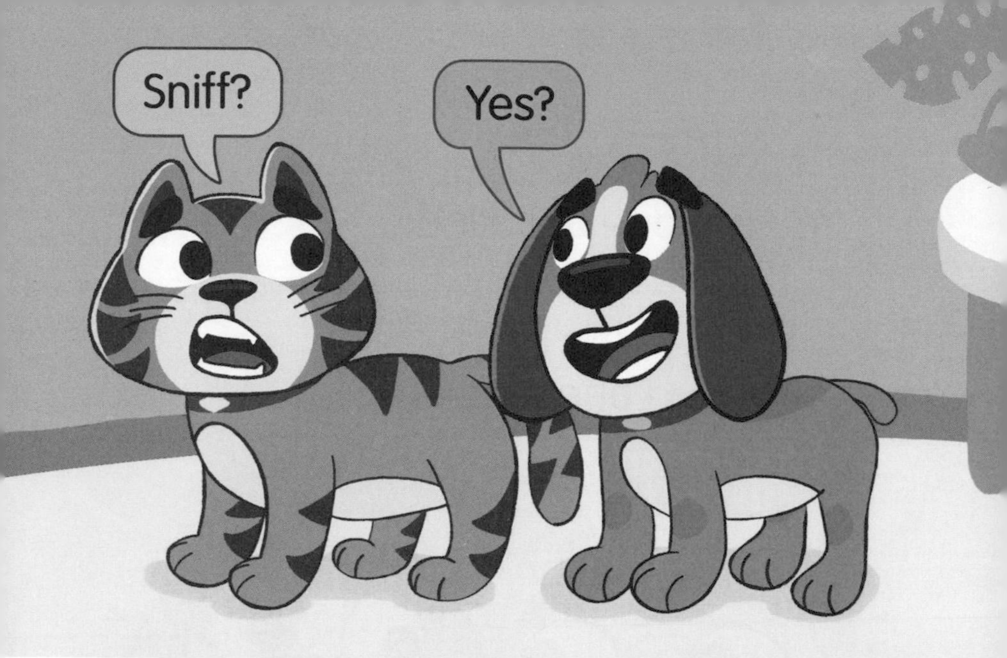
Sniff?
Yes?

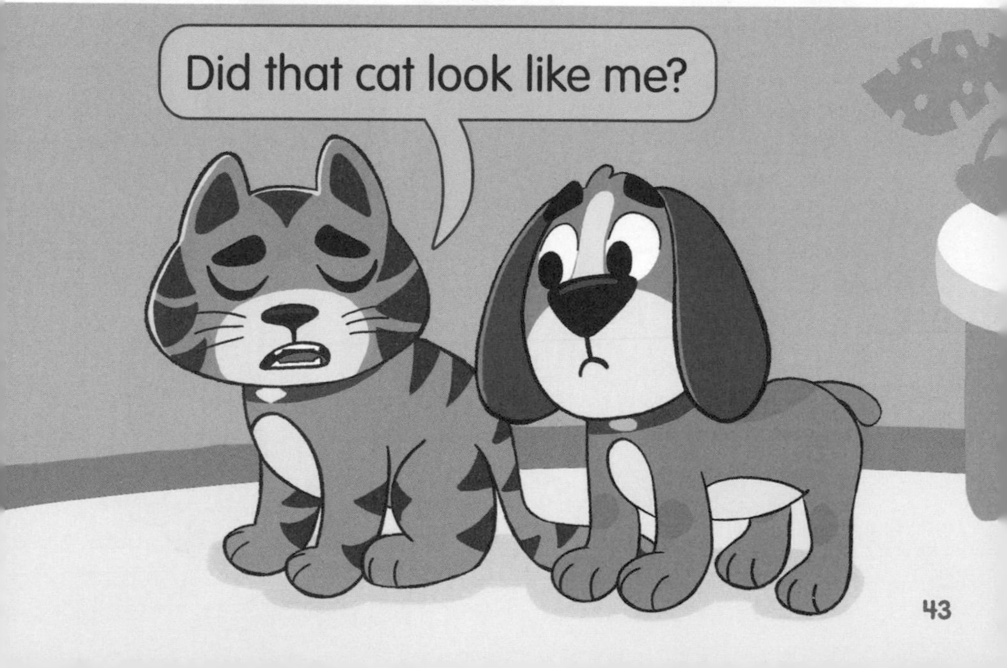
Did that cat look like me?

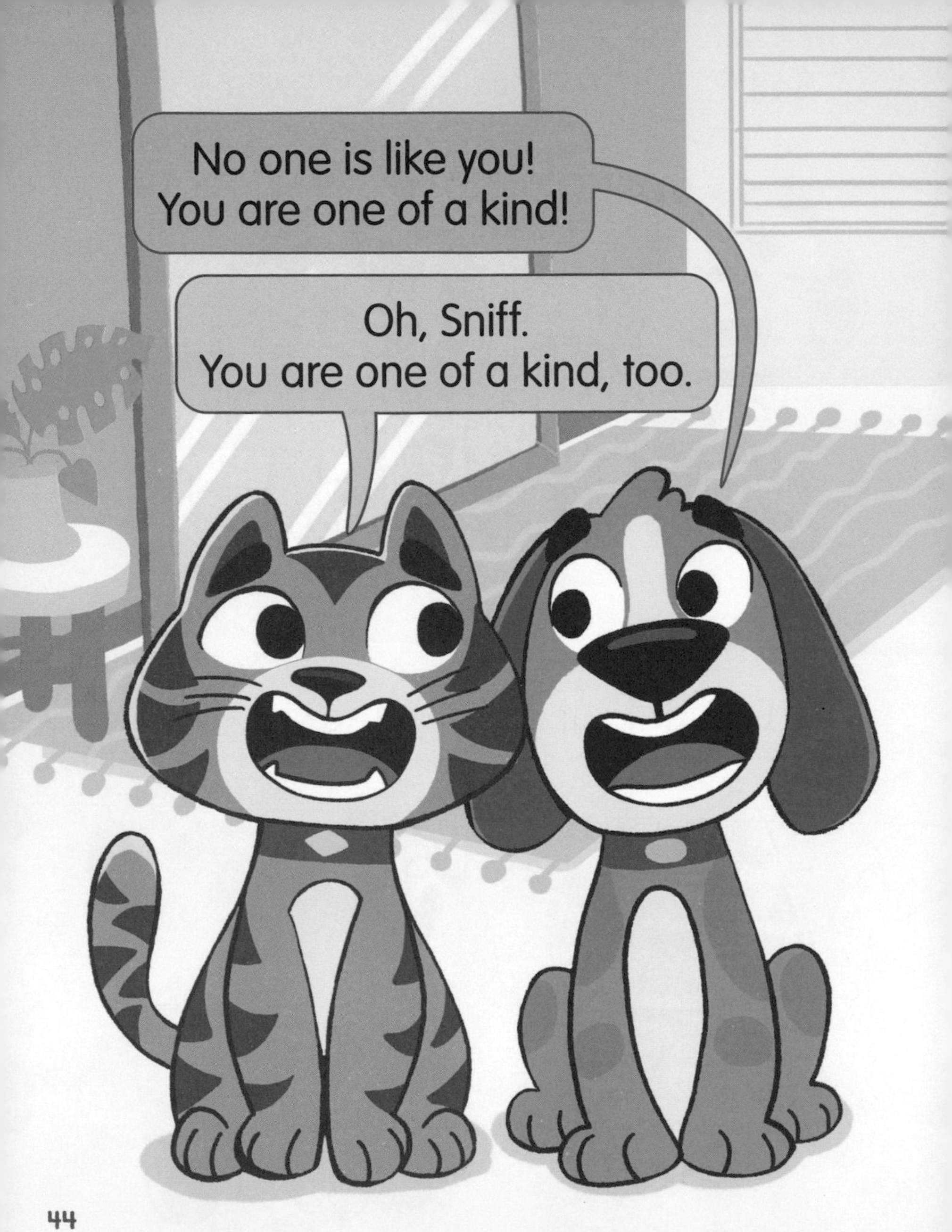
No one is like you! You are one of a kind!
Oh, Sniff. You are one of a kind, too.

About the Creators

Vicky Fang lives in Mountain View, California, with her husband, their two sons, a few sea monkeys, and one pet rhinoceros beetle. They are now considering what their next new pet might be. She is also the author of the Scholastic Branches early chapter book series Layla and the Bots.

Luisa Leal is originally from Venezuela, but she now calls Nevada home. There, she designs characters and backgrounds for games. Telling stories through pictures has always been her passion, and illustrating this series is a dream come true for her. When she's not drawing, you can find her swimming, riding her bike, or planning her next adventure!

YOU CAN DRAW SCRATCH!

1 Draw an oval for the head and two upside-down "V" shapes on top for the ears.

2 Draw Scratch's body and show the outline of all four paws. Then add a tail.

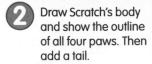

3 Draw two circles for the eyes and two triangles inside the ears. Draw one big circle for the face.

4 Add Scratch's pupils, nose, and collar. Next, draw Scratch's two front legs and two back paws.

5 Add eyebrows for expression. Draw stripes. Give Scratch whiskers and a smile!

6 Color in your drawing!

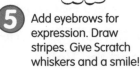

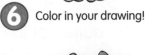

WHAT'S YOUR STORY?

Sniff and Scratch love pie!
Imagine **you** make a pie as a surprise for them.
What kind of pie would you make?
What would Sniff and Scratch say about it?
Write and draw your story!

scholastic.com/acorn